The Luck
of the
Buttons

The Luck
of the
Buttons

ANNE YLVISAKER

CANDLEWICK PRESS

Copyright © 2011 by Anne Ylvisaker

First edition 2011

Library of Congress Cataloging-in-Publication Data
Ylvisaker, Anne.
The luck of the Buttons / Anne Ylvisaker.
p. cm.
Summary: In Iowa circa 1929, spunky twelve-year-old Tugs vows to turn her family's luck around, with the help of a Brownie camera and a small-town mystery that only she can solve.
ISBN 978-0-7636-5066-7
[1. Friendship — Fiction. 2. Luck — Fiction. 3. Family life — Iowa — Fiction. 4. Photography — Fiction. 5. Iowa — History — 20th century — Fiction. 6. Mystery and detective stories.] I. Title.
PZ7.Y57Luc 2011
[Fic] — dc22
2010039169

11 12 13 14 15 16 BVG 10 9 8 7 6 5 4 3 2 1

Printed in Berryville, VA, U.S.A.

This book was typeset in Kennerly.

Candlewick Press
99 Dover Street
Somerville, Massachusetts 02144

visit us at www.candlewick.com

For Maria —
lucky me

Contents

The Luck

of the

Buttons

An Invitation

Tugs Button darted past Zip's Hardware, stumbled over the lunch specials sign at Al and Irene's Luncheonette, and pushed through the door of Ward's Ben Franklin as if the devil himself were chasing her. She ducked behind Aggie Millhouse and Aggie's mother, hissing, "Save me from the Rowdies!" as G.O. Lindholm burst in, looking around wildly.

Tugs sidled up close to Aggie, trying to melt into her back, and just as G.O. spotted her, Lester Ward, the oldest Ward boy, pointed at him from behind the register and hollered, "Out, Lindholm! Take your thieving fingers and get outa my father's store!"

"And stay out!" echoed his younger brother Burton, who was stocking the sundries shelves.

"You're such a Button," G.O. spat as he banged out the door.

"Button," mimicked Burton.

"G.O.'s not a Rowdy," said Aggie, turning to Tugs.

"But he wants to be, and wanting to be a hoodlum is almost the same thing as being a hoodlum, or worse, now that I think about it because what did the Rowdies ever do except lump around looking tough, whereas G.O. . . ." said Tugs. "You saved my hinder for sure."

Mrs. Millhouse gasped at Tugs's crass language, but Tugs was loquacious in her relief. "I popped the tire on his bike, but I didn't mean to. I mean, I was putting nails in the street just to stop, well, never mind. I see you got lots of fun things in your basket, Aggie. Looks like a party. Looks like your birthday. Twelve, huh? I turned twelve weeks ago. I would have invited you to my party, only it's an even year, and I only have parties on my odd birthdays, though they aren't really odd—ha, ha, ha! Guess you're going to have fun, huh?

"Look," she said, picking up a whistle out of Aggie's mother's basket. "Mrs. Millhouse, you are one mighty good mother to let your daughter have something as loud as whistles at her party."

Mrs. Millhouse stared dumbfounded as Tugs kept rambling, but Aggie interrupted.

"I've never stood quite this close to you before, Tugs. We are exactly the same height. And you came running in that door awfully fast. You gave me an idea."

That stopped Tugs midsentence. Aggie Millhouse, of the Millhouse Bank and Trust family, got an idea from her, Tugs Button, of the . . . just Button family? She wiped her nose on the inside of her arm, then across

3

the front of her overalls. She admired Aggie in her pressed dress and shiny shoes.

"You should be a dancer, Aggie, with your long legs and your long hair."

"I'd rather play basketball," said Aggie. "But listen to my idea. We should be partners for the three-legged race."

The Independence Day three-legged races were the stuff of legend in Goodhue. Children remembered the winning teams the way they remembered who won every Iowa Hawkeye football game. Tugs had been paired with her cousin Ned for the past hundred years, and she was resigned to the same fate this year.

"What about Felicity?" Tugs asked. "You always race with Felicity."

"She's going to Cedar Rapids for the auto races. Besides, we never win. Do you have a partner?"

Aggie's question took the fuel right out of Tugs's motor. It was assumed that she would run with Ned, but the words had never been spoken. Ned and Tugs had the same birthday one year apart, which made them kind of like twins, except that they had different parents and were born in different years. Tugs was an only child, so they'd grown up playing together by default. *Family first* was the Button credo.

They made an awkward pair, Ned and Tugs, he short, she tall, and being from nearly the same gene pool, neither one was blessed with coordination. She'd try to take shorter strides, he'd try to take longer strides, and they usually ended up in a lump about five feet from the start line. Buttons were not, as a rule, graceful.

Aggie Millhouse, with her straight teeth and wide circle of friends, would race with her, Tugs Button? Still, Ned was her cousin.

"Ned," she said.

"Do you have to?"

"Well, I . . . he's my cousin and you're . . . I mean, me and you, we never . . . and besides, it's next week."

"Yes, well," interrupted Mrs. Millhouse. "That's that, then. Come along, Aggie."

"Hmm," said Aggie, and pressed on. "What are you doing tomorrow afternoon?"

Tugs scratched her nose. "Probably just studying my belly button, as Granddaddy Ike says. He's really my *great* granddaddy, because he's the granddaddy of my own dad, but everyone calls him Granddaddy Ike."

Mrs. Millhouse raised her eyebrows at this outburst and put her arm around Aggie, leading her toward the door.

"You can do that another day," said Aggie. "Come to my birthday party. Two o'clock. Do you know where I live?"

The invitation rendered both Tugs and Mrs. Millhouse speechless, and before either could respond, Aggie and her mother were out of the store, leaving Tugs looking after them. Absently, she picked up a statuette of the real Ben Franklin and turned it over in her hands.

"Are you buying?" said Lester. This startled Tugs so that she dropped Ben, and as she stooped to pick up his separated head and body, Lester barked, "You break it, you buy it!" Tugs hastily deposited both pieces on the shelf and ducked out the door.

"Rapscallion!" Lester hollered after her.

Pie-Worthy

There was pie on the table when Tugs returned. Pie in the Button family meant trouble.

When Uncle Norton sliced off his left foot with the scythe while trying to mow hay for the horses after having gotten into the cups, the Buttons baked pie-plant pies and gathered at Uncle Norton and Uncle Elmer's farm to carry on about the sorry state of farm utensils and the difficulty of working the land. Now Uncle Norton spent his days sitting on the porch spitting sunflower shells over the rail while Uncle Elmer wrestled the farm by himself.

When a card-playing con man suckered Uncle Elmer out of his seed money and he had to plant with last year's leftovers, which he did too hastily, and a storm washed all those seeds away, the Buttons baked up oatmeal pies and cursed the queen of spades, Mother Nature, and even Mother Goose for good measure.

There were apple pies for fall funerals and custard pies for the measles, mumps, and broken bones. Fiona Button, like Aunt Mina and Tugs's own mother, technically only a Button by marriage, had once traveled all the way to Georgia and returned with a suitcase full of pecans begging to be baked into flaky crusts. It was nearly a month before anything pie-worthy happened, and when it did—marital trouble, Fiona and Albert—the pecans were passed around, and the family was together eating pecan pie for enough evenings in a row that Fiona and Albert called a truce and mended their differences.

Now not only was there pie on the table, but Aunt Mina was there with a fork in her hand and eight-year-old Gladdy by her side.

"Tugs Button. Where have you been? Your mother's been worried sick. Gladdy and I brought pie, and now I've got a mind to just take your piece straight on over to Uncle Wilson and let him eat it instead."

"But Aggie Millhouse asked . . . Pie?" said Tugs. "Did someone die? Where's Dad? Is Granddaddy Ike all right?"

Mother Button interrupted. "I'm not worried sick, Mina. I just said . . ." But Aunt Mina wasn't finished.

"Not only are you late, off getting up to who knows what kind of mischief, but my Ned is home moping because he's got no one to toss a ball with. And that, Tugs Esther Button, is your fault. With you off doing heaven knows what this morning, Ned tried to take up with Ralph Stump. And you know as well as I do that I won't let Ned cavort with a Stump. Next thing you know he'll be smoking cigarettes behind Zip's with the Rowdies. I knew I should have sent him to help Elmer on the farm this summer."

"Pie?" repeated Tugs.

"Mina dear, just because Mr. Stump . . ." tried Mother Button, but she was cut off again by Aunt Mina, who set down her fork and turned to face Tugs.

"Tugs. You're twelve. I'm going to tell it to you plain. This is butter-up pie. Mostly brown sugar, cream, and eggs, along with a dash of something from Uncle Wilson's cupboard. I'm sweetening your mama because your family has got to take Granny into your house. She's insulted Aunt Fiona for the last time, says Uncle Albert. She has to go. I've got Uncle Wilson and Ned and my little Gladdy here to manage, and with Granddaddy Ike living next door, well . . ."

Tugs looked at Mother Button, who shrugged and held out a fork.

"May as well fortify. We're driving over to Swisher soon as you eat your lunch."

11

Tugs looked around the compact quarters of the Button house. There was one deep room, with a sitting area at the front, kitchen at the back, and dining table between the two. A pair of bedrooms opened off one side, with a bathroom between them.

"Where are we going to put her?"

Aunt Mina jumped in before Mother Button had a chance to answer. "There will be time enough to worry about that once she's here. Now, eat up, child. We're waiting on you." She grabbed Gladdy's empty plate and slid a piece of pie onto it for Tugs. "Oh, and there was a boy here looking for you. M.G.? T.L.?"

"It was G.O. Lindholm," said Gladdy primly, folding her arms across her chest. "He said you'd know what it was about."

Stranger in a Panama Hat

Granny fell asleep the moment the automobile started moving, like a baby rocked in a cradle. "How'm I supposed to learn to drive one of these danged things if I can't stay awa . . ." she began as they put her in the backseat with Gladdy and set off.

They passed out of Swisher into the country. Tugs and Ned rode in the open air of the rumble seat, but Tugs didn't notice the hawk swooping overhead or the fox darting up to the edge of the road then back between the low stalks of early corn. What if Lester Ward made her pay for the statue she'd broken? What if Aggie found out and didn't want her to come to her party after all?

Ned interrupted her thoughts. "Fourth of July next week," he said.

"Huh?"

"IndePENdence Day," he said a little louder, and Tugs's stomach fell further. How could she tell him she wanted to run the three-legged with Aggie?

"We aren't going to win, are we?" Ned continued.

"Nope."

"That's OK. I just like to race. I can't catch a football, but I still like to play."

"Yup."

Tugs played over her encounter with Aggie in her head. What if there was a chance of winning? What if she did run with Aggie? She felt a wave of guilt for even thinking it. Buttons considered victory, even for one's affiliated party in national politics, showing off.

Don't go getting a swell head, was all her father had said when Tugs won the first round of the third-grade spelling bee. She'd been sure to confuse a letter here or there after that.

Ned and Tugs watched a cow trying to break out of its fence and a mare drinking from the cow pond. They passed a man in a Panama hat, walking on the side of the road. He waved, but Aunt Mina was driving fast and rounded a curve before Tugs and Ned could wave back.

"Where's Granny going to sleep?" Ned asked.

"Davenport."

"Where are you going to sit?"

"Kitchen, I guess."

"Closer to the cookie jar, anyhow," said Ned.

"Mm-hmm."

Just then the car sputtered. They slowed, then lurched and rumbled to the side of the road and stopped. Tugs and Ned peered in the back window. Aunt Mina was climbing out of the car. Granny had popped awake and was shaking her finger at Gladdy.

Tugs and Ned hopped out and walked around to Aunt Mina and Mother Button, who were pondering the hood. Granny banged on the door.

"Gladdy, keep Granny in the car!" Aunt Mina hollered, but Granny batted Gladdy's hand away and appealed to Ned and Tugs through the open window.

"Help the old lady out of this rattletrap!"

Tugs and Ned opened the door and each grabbed one of Granny's skinny arms and helped her climb down. Gladdy passed Granny's cane to Ned, then climbed out herself.

"You're going to be in trouble!" Gladdy taunted, but they ignored her. Gladdy was always trying to get them in trouble.

"Look!" Gladdy said. "Someone's coming."

"What?" asked Aunt Mina sharply. "Where?"

"She's right. A man," said Tugs. "Walking this way."

"Everyone back in the car," commanded

Aunt Mina. "It's probably a hobo or maybe a gangster, and here we are, women alone in the middle of nowhere."

"Hey!" protested Ned. "I'm not a woman."

"Pshaw," spat Granny. "There's six of us and just one of him. He looks like a scrawny fellow, anyhow. We can take him."

"Is that a Panama? Hoboes don't wear straw hats," said Mother Button as the man got closer. She straightened her own hat and smoothed her skirt. "Try to look respectable, everyone. Maybe he knows something about cars."

"I'll find out," said Ned. He ran to meet the man as he approached.

"Ned!" Aunt Mina shouted after him. "You come back here this instant!" But Ned kept running.

"I stayed right here, Mother, no matter how curious I am," said Gladdy.

"I'll go with Ned," said Tugs, and she dashed off before anyone could protest.

17

The man was looking down at Ned and talking intently as Tugs approached. He did not look like a hobo or a murderer. He was younger than the uncles, wearing a dapper suit, tie loosed at the neck, and carrying a leather satchel.

"Who are you and what are you doing out here?" Tugs demanded.

The man laughed.

"He's our newspaperman," said Ned. "He got off the train at the wrong station and no one was there to pick him up and he's been walking all day. He came all the way from Chicago."

"We don't have a newspaper anymore," said Tugs.

The man chuckled. "You are an observant one, aren't you?" he said. "You're right, of course, but you're going to have a newspaper." He tipped his hat. "Harvey Moore, bringing progress to Iowa one town at a time. Pleased to make your acquaintance."

"Goodhue men don't wear fancy hats,

except for Mr. Pepper, who is a snappy dresser, and Mayor Corbett."

"That so?" Mr. Moore laughed.

"My aunt thinks you're going to murder us," said Tugs.

"So young Ned tells me. With all this dust and grime, I may look a bit shady today, but I assure you, the only murdering I'll be doing is of lunch, soon as I can find it. I haven't had anything to eat since the train left the Windy City."

"We've got sandwiches," said Ned. "And pie."

"Now, that's the way to welcome a new-comer, sport," said Harvey, plopping his hat on Ned's head and walking toward the car. Tugs stood back and watched them go. He didn't look like a newspaperman, but then she'd never known a newspaperman in person.

The women were huddled around the front of the car, where Aunt Mina was heaving open the hood.

Harvey flashed his winning smile and introduced himself all around.

"Your lucky day, ladies. I worked as a mechanic back when. What seems to be the problem?" he asked.

"It just made a chortling sound, then sputtered to a stop," said Aunt Mina.

"It was more like a *whirrawhoop*," said Mother Button.

"*Clank* was all I heard," said Granny.

Gladdy just stood there and giggled. She combed her fingers through her hair and giggled some more.

"Pull yourself together, Gladdy, and get the nice man a sandwich," admonished Aunt Mina, smoothing her own hair and straightening her collar. Gladdy reached through the window to the basket on the backseat, then bumped her head backing out, which threw her into another fit of giggles.

Tugs stood off to the side. She held her fingers out in a square, like a camera lens.

She watched her mother and Aunt Mina watch Harvey peer under the hood. She watched Ned trying to work his way in front of Granny and Granny nudging him out of the way with her cane. She watched Gladdy hover around the edge, clutching two sandwiches. Everyone was bending, straightening, standing, sitting.

"When he's done with the heart of the beast, an old lady could use a hand getting into the shade of the automobile," Granny said.

Tugs wondered what Aggie Millhouse would do if she were here. For a mechanic, Mr. Moore didn't seem to be fixing anything very quickly. Aggie wouldn't giggle, like Gladdy, in the face of that broad smile and smooth talk; that was certain.

Tugs climbed into the front seat and felt around underneath, where she'd seen her father stash the manual. She paged through until she found what she was looking for, then stowed it back where she'd found it. She walked around to the hood, where everyone was gathered.

"I know what's the matter," she said.

"Shush, child," said Aunt Mina. "Can't you see Mr. Moore is trying to repair our automobile?"

"But I . . ." said Tugs.

"Hush!" echoed Granny.

"No, no," Harvey said, straightening and looking directly at Tugs. "Our little lady is dressed like a mechanic in those overalls; we'd better listen to her." He laughed.

Tugs looked down at her pants. "Mechanics wear coveralls," she muttered.

"What's that?" snapped Aunt Mina.

Tugs had seen her father work on the car a hundred times. He'd chattered while he worked, telling her everything he knew about the engine and how cars worked.

"We're out of gas," she said simply.

Harvey Moore smiled even more broadly and snatched his Panama off Ned's head, settling it back on his own.

"Truth be told, I was always better with a football than a wrench," he said. "Played for Purdue, back in . . . But you're not interested in . . ."

"Yes, we are!" said Ned. "Did you ever play Iowa?"

"Ned," said Aunt Mina. "Let the man finish."

"As missy was saying, you're out of gas," said Harvey. "Look how long you have had the hood open. I actually just assumed you knew you were out of gas. I am checking the safety of the valves and the . . . well . . . as soon as I have a little fuel myself, as they say, I'll skedaddle to fetch you lovely ladies a can of gas so you can be on your way."

Gladdy thrust two sandwiches out to Harvey, and Aunt Mina reached into her skirt pocket and pressed some coins into his hand.

"Hope he brings you the change," snapped Granny as they watched Harvey saunter off. "That looked to me like more than enough for a can of gas, Mina, and now we've given him Ned and Gladdy's sandwiches."

"Hey!" said Gladdy and Ned together.

"The sandwiches are all the same. How do you know they were ours?" said Ned.

"Well, I'm an old lady. It wouldn't be my sandwich, now, would it? And your mother is driving. Couldn't be her sandwich or Auntie Corrine's, now, either, 'cause she's doing the navigating. Can't be Tugs's sandwich, because Tugs helped Mr. Moore solve the mystery of the automobile. So it must be your and Gladdy's sandwiches. Now, go make yourselves scarce. Tugs and me want to dine in relative tranquility."

Tugs accepted the sandwich Granny handed her, but as she took a bite, she felt a little guilty. She tore it in three parts and handed a piece each to Gladdy and Ned.

They didn't have to wait long for help. Lester Ward's roadster came speeding along presently, with Harvey Moore in the passenger seat. Tugs slid down in the backseat, hoping desperately that Lester wouldn't see her there.

"Rescued!" she heard Harvey bellow. "I flagged down this fine fellow, and isn't he the good Samaritan, picking up a stranger in need and buying a can of gas for you lovely ladies besides. There. And look, he's filling it for you, too."

As Lester finished, Harvey clapped him on the back. "Let's go, my friend. We'll leave the ladies to their journey."

"Wait!" Ned hollered. "Can I ride with you?"

Tugs peered over the seat. She saw Harvey take a long drink of lemonade from a bottle in Lester's car as they sped off, Ned waving from the center of the road until they were out of sight.

"Isn't he just the most amazing young man?" said Aunt Mina.

"He's dashing," gushed Gladdy.

"Imagine," continued Aunt Mina. "Bringing the newspaper back to Goodhue. It's about time."

"Harvey Moore," said Mother Button. "That's the name of someone who can get something done."

"He dresses too fancy for a mechanic or a football player," said Tugs.

"Tugs, where have you been? He's a newspaperman," said Aunt Mina. "Now, everyone back in the car. Granny's exhausted."

Made to Order

Aggie's birthday party would be a whiz-bang affair, Tugs was certain, much fancier than her own parties, which were always just family and usually ended with something or someone breaking. Last year Grand-daddy Ike fell off the front porch with a plate of cake in his hand. He landed on Gladdy, which broke his fall but bruised her up something awful and shattered one of Mother Button's five remaining china plates.

Tugs combed her hair for the occasion of Aggie's party and put on her other pair of overalls. She tiptoed into the living room, where Granny was napping.

"Are you sure you're invited?" whispered Mother Button as Tugs laced her shoes.

"Sure I'm sure."

"I suppose I've got something you could wrap up for a gift." Mother Button rooted around in her whatnot drawer and pulled out a nearly new pincushion.

"Does Aggie do handwork?" she asked.

"Don't think so," said Tugs.

"Hmm . . ." said Mother Button, continuing to search. She opened cupboards and drawers, then looked between the sofa cushions.

"She likes active things," said Tugs. "She's good at running and jumping. I know what to do," she said, and ran out to the shed, coming back with a coil of twine. "Can you help me braid real fast? I always get it twisted."

"Well . . ." said Mother Button, but Tugs was already laying down a long line of twine across the kitchen floor. She went for the

28

scissors, cut it, and measured out two more the same length.

"See?" said Tugs. Her mother did not see.

"We'll just braid this up and tie some big loops at the end and it will be a brand-new jump rope. She'll love it."

Mother Button looked at the clock. "You're going to be late, Tugs. And I don't know . . ."

"Please," begged Tugs. "I'll even let you braid it. You braid your hair every blame day. I'll hold the end."

"OK, then," sighed Mother Button as she picked up the three ends and knotted them together. "Hold tight." So Tugs sat in one kitchen chair holding one end while Mother Button sat in another tossing one edge strand over the middle strand and then the other.

"Left, right, left, right!" cheered Tugs.

"You're going to wake Granny," said Mother Button, and Tugs hushed. She was going to Aggie Millhouse's birthday party. There would be cake and games and girls all her age. For a moment she felt uncertain; a little flutter rustled in her stomach, but then Mother Button stood up.

"Done. One jump rope made to order." She went to her room and got a hair ribbon, wound up the jump rope, and tied it with the ribbon. "There you go. Now, do you want me to walk you to Aggie's?"

"Mother!" gasped Tugs. "No! Everyone knows where the Millhouses live."

"Well, OK, then. Steer clear of hooligans. Say thank you. And please. And don't be the last one to leave."

"I won't!"

Tugs paused on the front step, looking down the street both ways for signs of G.O. Lindholm. The street and sidewalk were quiet, but there was Harvey Moore, walking out of the Dostals' next door in a snappy navy suit, straightening his tie as he whistled his way down the front walk. He stopped to check his reflection in the window of Mr. Dostal's Model T and would have whistled his way right past Tugs had she not spoken up.

"Mr. Moore!" she called, walking toward him. "What are you doing at the Dostals'?"

Harvey kept walking.

"Mr. Moore!" Tugs called again. This time he turned around.

"Oh! Guess I didn't hear you. Hi there, uh . . . Helen?"

"Tugs," said Tugs. "Tugs Button. You . . . helped us with our car yesterday."

"Right! Right-o. Yes, siree. The car. Running fine now, is it?"

"I guess," said Tugs. She was torn between wanting to know what Mr. Moore was up to and wanting to get to Aggie's on time.

"Right. Right-o," repeated Mr. Moore. "Yes, well. I better be getting on, then. Run along."

"Why were you at the Dostals'?" said Tugs.

"They've rented me a room until I find

31

my own place, if you must know," said Harvey. He pasted on a grin. "That Mrs. Dostal is a sweetheart, yes, siree." He turned and walked down the sidewalk.

"First time I've heard her called that," Tugs said, catching up with him as he was walking her way.

"Where are you going now?" she asked.

"To the newspaper office, of course."

"We don't have a newspaper office. People here read the *Cedar Rapids Tribune.* I've got pictures from it on my wall."

"The *Cedar Rapids Tribune.* That's just the problem. Goodhue folks should be getting Goodhue news."

"If you're headed downtown, you're going the wrong way," said Tugs.

Harvey stopped and looked at Tugs. He wasn't smiling.

"I . . ." he started, then stopped and grinned, all teeth. "Right you are, missy. You are quite the know-it-all, aren't you? A fellow new in town has to feel his way around. I'll just be on my way, then," he said, and turned abruptly and walked the other way.

"Turn right at the corner!" Tugs hollered after him, but Harvey just waved without looking back and continued straight on.

Party Games

Behind the screen, the door with its brass lion's head knocker stood open. Tugs didn't know if she was supposed to open the screen to reach the knocker or if she should knock on the screen door itself or simply shout *yoo-hoo,* as was her habit when she was running into familiar houses. There was a doorbell, but she couldn't make herself press it. She could hear squeals and laughter.

She moved over to the window and peered in. A stack of beautifully wrapped gifts, all in boxes with bows and with cards in envelopes, was piled on the dining-room table. She supposed the largest, prettiest box was from Felicity Anderson. The Marys were probably there, too.

Tugs looked down at the braided twine in her hand. She took a step backward. What if Aggie was already regretting having invited her? What if Tugs had understood it all wrong and Aggie hadn't really invited her? That had to be it. She could leave now and no one would have to know she'd even been there. She'd tell Aggie that a bee had stung her — no, that she'd stepped on a bee and it had stung the bottom of her foot, so she couldn't walk for twenty-four hours.

But as she reached the steps, she heard Mr. Millhouse bellow, "Aggie, there's another girl here! Go welcome her in."

Tugs was caught. She dropped the jump rope over the porch rail into the bushes and put on her company face. "Hiya, Aggie!" she said. "Happy birthday. Just swinging by to say that. Happy birthday, that is. Twelve. Huh."

"Come on!" said Aggie, opening the door and pulling Tugs inside. "You're late, but never mind. There's still cake. And we just started games."

Tugs ate a piece of cake, sitting on the edge of a kitchen chair. The other girls were in the backyard, and Mrs. Millhouse was at the sink, washing the cake dishes, one eye on Tugs. Tugs was surprised to find that the cake was actually pretty dry and not as good as the cakes her own mother made. It was a revelation. Tugs had assumed that tastier food came out of fancier houses. When she stood up, a shower of crumbs fell from her lap to the floor.

"Thanks for the cake, Mrs. Millhouse," Tugs said, bringing her plate to the sink. "You might try an extra egg next time. That's what my mother does, and her cake doesn't leave as many crumbles."

"Well, I never!" gasped Mrs. Millhouse as Tugs stepped out the back door to the yard, where the games were under way.

Tugs hesitated, then nudged her way into the circle of girls.

The girls had already played pin-the-tail-on-the-donkey, which featured a genuine store-bought paper donkey, and were about to begin the beanbag toss. Aggie put one hand over her eyes and with the other reached into a large basket and chose a bright gingham bag.

"Red!" she cried. "I was hoping for red. Everyone gets to keep their beanbag, so I hope you get the color you like." She passed the basket to Felicity, who drew a yellow beanbag, and on around the circle.

Tugs giggled with nervous excitement. She hoped she'd get a red one, like Aggie. She would impress Aggie by tossing her bag in the hole on the first try. Aggie would say, "That's my friend Tugs. Isn't she good at party games? I asked her to race the three-legged with me." And a prize. Maybe there would be a prize. A whistle.

Tugs watched as Mary Louise and Mary Helen each drew pink bags and squealed with the thrill of drawing the same color, never mind that Mary Helen had peeked to ensure the match. Tugs rubbed her damp hands on her pants leg. Couldn't they hurry it up? Was there another red bag?

Then it was just Mary Alice and Tugs left. Mary Alice barely had her hand out of the basket before Tugs grabbed it from her, more eagerly than she'd intended, causing Mary Alice to drop her beanbag on the ground. Aggie's dog, Mitten, scampered over, grabbed it in his mouth, and trotted off.

"Well!" exclaimed Mary Alice. "Isn't that just typical? Remember when Tugs knocked you into that coat hook in third grade, Felicity? You'll have that scar over your eye forever!"

Tugs flushed and dropped the basket as she jumped up to help Aggie chase Mitten. But Mitten was under the fence and off down the block, and Aggie turned back with a shrug.

"Don't worry, Aggie — I'll get him!" Tugs

hollered as she flung open the gate and followed Mitten.

Mitten ran a straight line down the block, then rounded the corner and ran catty-corner across the street and into Liberty Park. Tugs slowed to scoop up the lavender beanbag that was leaking beans through the hole Mitten's teeth had punctured, waited for a car to pass, then stopped, one foot off the curb.

There was Mitten, barking and running circles around Luther Tingvold, Bess McCrea, and Walter Williams. The Rowdies. Tugs lifted her foot out of the street and backed behind a tree. Had they seen her?

She peered through the low branches. Finn and Frankie Chacey were there, too, sitting atop the jungle gym, tossing a ball back and forth to Walter, who was a moving target on a swing. Mitten yelped and weaved around the Rowdies. Bess lit up a cigarette and passed it to Luther. G.O. wasn't there, but Tugs was sure he'd soon show up and try to join in. She looked down at the beanbag, now nearly empty of beans and damp from her sweaty hand.

"Mitten," she whispered. With one last glance to be sure the Rowdies weren't looking her way, Tugs ran back around the corner, then slowed to a walk toward Aggie's, where the girls had gathered in the front yard to watch for Mitten's return.

Tugs stuffed the lavender beanbag into her pocket and said, "You can have my beanbag, Mary Alice."

"I already used it," replied Mary Alice, holding up a red bag. "And I won, so thank you very much." She held up her prize, which hung around her neck, a whistle on a thin red ribbon.

"You're welcome," said Tugs weakly.

Aggie's mother came out on the porch just then. "Time for presents," she called. "Come inside, girls. Mitten will come home when he's ready."

Tugs stood in the yard and watched the girls tromp up the steps.

"Aggie, I got to go," Tugs said. "Sorry I ruined your party."

"You didn't . . ." Aggie started, but Tugs was already to the sidewalk and off at a trot.

"Don't forget the three-legged!" Aggie called after her. "We need to practice!"

Progress

It was too soon to go home. Granny would quiz her about the Millhouse home and why was she back so fast and did something happen? Her feet found their way to the library.

The Goodhue library had the largest dictionary Tugs had ever seen. It sat on its own small table on a high pedestal. There were pictures next to some of the words. A girl could learn the most amazing things.

Like that a goat was not only an animal, but also the person who caused their team to lose. You wouldn't think Ralph Stump would have much of a vocabulary, but he had called Tugs a goat when she tripped over third base in the end-of-the-school-year kickball game in May, costing the sixth grade the tying run against the fifth grade.

And that a bonbon was a candy with a creamy center and a soft covering (as of chocolate). Granddaddy Ike was like a bonbon, with his silky, deep old-man voice and his soft, wrinkly skin. Milk baths, he said, were the key to soft skin.

Tugs used to think that everyone's name was in the dictionary, and when she had realized it was only hers, both *Tugs* and *Button,* she felt suddenly fond and possessive of it, as if this book were put here for her guidance alone. She found herself occasionally miffed when other people were using it. This afternoon, though, it was available for her perusal.

In the last two days, Tugs had gotten on the wrong side of G.O., broken Ben Franklin, been reprimanded by Harvey Moore, ruined Mary Alice's beanbag, and lost Aggie Millhouse's dog. Lester had called her a rapscallion. Maybe if she knew exactly what that was she could change her course before the Independence Day picnic.

> **Rapscallion:** a rascal; a scamp; a good-for-nothing fellow.

Rascal was on the next page: *a mean trickish fellow; a cheeky child; a rogue; a scoundrel; a trickster.*

Tugs colored, lifting a hand to her face. She was not a cheeky child. She flipped to *rogue.*

> **Rogue:** a vagrant; an idle, sturdy beggar; a vagabond; a tramp.

"What's the word?" asked Miss Lucy in her quiet library voice, coming up behind Tugs.

"Oh!" said Tugs a little too loudly. "Nothing!" She slapped the book shut and hopped off the stool.

Miss Lucy, the librarian, was the most exotic person of Tugs's acquaintance. Unmarried, yet not a widow or an old maid, taller even than Uncle Elmer, with wavy sunset-orange hair skimming her belt and a warm whispery voice, she seemed completely unaware of Tugs's lack of academic prowess whenever she chose books for her.

"The Independence Day patriotic essays are due tomorrow," Miss Lucy said. "How is yours coming?"

Tugs looked around to see whom Miss Lucy was talking to, and when she realized she was addressing her, Tugs Button, about writing an essay for a contest, she laughed. Out loud. In the library. No fewer than six people shushed Tugs, but Miss Lucy put her arm around Tugs's shoulder and led her to the library office.

"Here," Miss Lucy said. "You can use my desk. Just write a page on what you think about our good old U.S. of A. First thing that comes to mind. Oh, and a word to the wise. Our judges, Mrs. Winthrop and Miss Potter, are quite excited about the idea of *progress,* after talking to the man from Chicago who is going to start up a newspaper right here in Goodhue, once he raises the funds for a printing press. Imagine that, Tugs. It will be called the *Goodhue Progress*. Progress. Now, that would make a nice theme for an essay, wouldn't it?"

Tugs was not familiar with being asked what she thought about anything. What *did* she think about the United States? Tugs looked around the library office. She picked up the small dictionary Miss Lucy kept on her desk and looked up the word *progress*. She studied the portrait of President Hoover hanging on the wall and felt a swell of pride.

When she came out of the office, she felt suddenly shy, and to cover it up, she said roughly, "It's stupid. Don't read it." Then she dropped it in the trash and walked slowly to the door, glancing back and hoping Miss Lucy would retrieve it from the can.

My favorite thing about the United States of America is our new president because he is from Iowa like me. I have been to West Branch where Herbert Hoover was born. The houses in West Branch look like the houses in Goodhue. When he was a boy Herbert Hoover sledded on hills in winter like children in Goodhue do and in summer he fished the streams like we do.

During the Great War he helped get food to hungry people in Europe, and in America he taught people to conserve food.

My Granddaddy Ike and all his friends wrote letters to Herbert Hoover to ask him to run for president. Herbert Hoover solves problems, they said.

The dictionary says progress means moving forward. Herbert Hoover was just a boy in Iowa. Then he lived all over the world helping solve problems. Now he is president of the United States. That is progress. And Iowa is part of progress. So I am part of progress.

In Step

Monday morning, Tugs stayed indoors with *Rootabaga Stories,* trying to avoid Granny, who was in the backyard making war with weeds, and G.O., who was surely out looking for his revenge for the tire incident. She turned the pages, but her eyes were on the front window.

They used to be friends, she and G.O. In third and fourth grade. He was really good at drawing maps, and they'd plotted out a new town. She couldn't remember now what they'd named it, but it had three movie theaters and a racetrack, and each of their houses occupied the space of an entire block. Then his dad went to prison for robbery, and his mother took up making sculptures from junk, and G.O. had come back to school in the fall of fifth grade thin and mean.

Tugs jumped when she saw a head appear in the window and then at the front door. Aggie Millhouse was standing at her very house, on the other side of her very screen door. Tugs got up so fast, she tripped over her mother's darning basket, grabbed the floor lamp, which offered no stability, and sprawled with a thud face-first in front of the door.

"Ouch," said Aggie. "Can I come in?"

Tugs looked up, her hand on her nose.

"How did you get here?" she asked.

"I walked," said Aggie, letting herself in the door and helping Tugs up. They righted the lamp and tried to straighten its shade. The brightness of Aggie's navy-and-white sailor dress made the room around her look tired and worn.

"I mean," said Tugs, "how did you know where I live?"

"Mrs. Dostal does my mother's sewing. Sometimes I ride along when she drops it off. I saw you once when I was waiting in the Buick."

"Does your mother know you're here?"

"Nope. I'm supposed to be practicing piano. She was on the phone and I set a roll on the player piano. But as soon as the roll runs out, she'll know I'm not in there and start looking for me. She'd never think of coming here, though."

"Are you going to get in trouble?" asked Tugs.

"Nah," said Aggie. "Come on. We've got work to do. Can you walk?"

Tugs's knees smarted and her nose was sore, but she nodded.

"But you don't want to race with me."

"Sure I do. We are the exact same height," said Aggie. "Our legs are the same length; that's the secret to winning the three-legged. We don't have to be the fastest. We just have to step together. It's always the team

50

that doesn't fall down that wins. So that's what we need to practice, not falling down."

"That *will* take practice," said Tugs. Then another thought struck her. "What am I going to tell Ned?"

"Well, he must have some friends his own age. Maybe he wants to race with someone else, too, and just didn't want to hurt your feelings. Isn't there a Stump in his grade?"

Tugs had never thought of that possibility. Ned looked up to her because she was one year older. She just assumed that Ned wanted to do everything she did, because he was, well, Ned.

"I guess it wouldn't hurt to practice."

"Good," said Aggie. "Here, I found this braided twine in the bushes in my front yard. We could cut off part of it to tie around our ankles."

"No!" said Tugs. "I mean, that looks like a perfectly good jump rope, doesn't it? I'd hate to cut up someone's jump rope." And to prove the point, Tugs took the twine and tried to demonstrate its superior rope-jumping qualities. But on the first turn, she tripped. The rope was too short.

"Guess it's meant for someone shorter than us." Tugs looked at the rope for a moment. She pulled it through her hand. "If we wrapped it around our legs a few times, we wouldn't have to cut it."

"OK," said Aggie. "Come on."

Tugs was reluctant to go outside, in case of G.O. coming around. But here was Aggie Millhouse, wanting to race with her.

"Let's try the alley instead of the sidewalk," said Tugs. Aggie shrugged and followed Tugs out the back door. They sat on the step and tied their inside ankles together, then stood up.

They put their inside arms at each other's waists so they could stand shoulder to shoulder. Aggie smelled clean, and Tugs counted back in her head the number of days since she'd last taken a bath. She hoped Aggie couldn't tell.

Tugs glanced over at Aggie. They really were exactly the same height.

Buttons weren't generally tall, but Tugs had gotten height from her mother's side and had had her growth spurt early. When, in the third grade, someone had mistaken her for a sixth grader, she'd been mortified. What if people thought she was really twelve, but she was acting like an eight-year-old? At least now, with Aggie Millhouse just as tall, Tugs felt like she was the right height for her age. Aggie was fast. Maybe she could be, too.

"First we should practice just walking," said Aggie. "We'll always lead with our inside legs. The ones that are tied together. Ready, set, walk."

They took one step with their tied-together feet, but Aggie took a shortish step and Tugs eagerly tried to take a longer stride and fell forward, dragging Aggie to the ground, too.

"Are you hurt?" gasped Tugs. Had she broken Aggie Millhouse already? "And your dress!"

"I'm fine," said Aggie, brushing off her knees and turning so Tugs could inspect her dress.

"No tears, but it is pretty dirty."

"Overalls would be more convenient," sighed Aggie. "Maybe we should try something different. Let's count. Our together legs will be *one,* and our outside legs will be *two.*"

She pulled Tugs up and they tried again, counting out loud as they went. *One, two, one, two* . . . They were looking at their feet and concentrating so hard, they didn't hear G.O. running up behind them.

He shoved Tugs and Aggie hard, laughing as they fell. He stood over them as they untied their legs and tried to pull each other to standing.

"Quit being such a bully," said Aggie. Tugs gasped at Aggie's boldness.

"Who's going to make me?" said G.O., glaring at Tugs. "I'm the one with the busted bike."

Tugs stared back at G.O. He didn't look so scary when she stood next to Aggie. In fact, he looked about the same as in fourth grade, only taller with a surlier face. Tugs took a wavering breath. "Can't you just put a patch on it? It wasn't on purpose."

"It's more fun to watch you squirm," he said, and sauntered away.

"Rapscallion!" Tugs yelled after him.

"Never mind him," Aggie said. "We're getting the hang of this. Let's go faster."

They walked up and down the alley, then around the block, chanting *one, two, one, two* and keeping their eyes peeled for G.O.

"Maybe if we win, we'll get our name in the Goodhue paper," said Aggie.

"You know about the newspaper, too?"

"Sure. There was a man over for dinner last night."

"Harvey Moore?"

"Uh-huh. He asked my dad for money to get a printing press."

"Is he going to give it to him?"

"Yes. He thinks Mr. Moore has a good business plan."

Tugs concentrated on her *one, two, one, two*. If Mr. Millhouse thought it was a good plan . . .

"Didn't you think . . . ?" started Tugs, but just as they rounded the corner by Tugs's house, they heard the rumble of a car behind them. They turned to see Mrs. Millhouse at the wheel, hollering as she screeched to a halt.

"Agnes Lorraine Millhouse, you get in the car this instant." Aggie bent down to untie their ankles.

"And as for you, Tugs Button, you get on home. You should be ashamed of yourself, luring my Aggie away from the piano. You are a bad influence. Imagine what could have happened to her on the way over here."

"Don't worry, Mrs. Millhouse," said Tugs. "We're going to win the three-legged race on the Fourth of July! Aggie's a real good runner. And I can come over and help her practice the piano double tomorrow."

But Mrs. Millhouse wasn't paying attention to Tugs. She was already berating Aggie as she climbed into the car.

"Look out!" Aggie called out the window as Mrs. Millhouse sped off. Tugs spun around and saw G.O. running toward her. Tugs grabbed the rope off the ground and ran for home, leaving the sidewalk and cutting across lawns.

Mrs. Dostal appeared on her front porch just then, with a watering can. Tugs ran toward her.

"Good morning, Mrs. Dostal," said Tugs, stopping short at the fence between their houses.

Mrs. Dostal looked up.

"Tsk," she said. "So unladylike."

G.O. slunk by, scowling at Tugs as he passed.

"Rogue!" Tugs hollered after him. "Rascal! Scamp! Cheeky child!" Then she turned back to Mrs. Dostal.

"So," said Tugs in her most conversational tone. "You've got Mr. Moore living with you."

"Yes," said Mrs. Dostal. "We take in boarders now and again. You know that, Tugs."

"Don't you think there's something fishy about him?" asked Tugs.

Mrs. Dostal lifted her watering can and held it to her bosom. "Why, Tugs Button. What kind of nonsense is that? Mr. Moore is a perfectly gentlemanly gentleman. He's going to bring the *news* to Goodhue. *Progress,* it's going to be called. The *Goodhue Progress.* He's going to go to church with us every Sunday he's here, he says. And in exchange for room and board, he's going to fix Mr. Dostal's car and teach him how to sail. Besides, I don't know why I'm telling this to an eleven-year-old."

"I'm twelve," said Tugs.

"Twelve, then," huffed Mrs. Dostal. "Now, if you can't say anything nice . . ." And she resumed her watering.

Tugs pressed on. "Is he really not paying you room and board?"

"Why, child, I just told you. He's paying *in kind.* That's what some people do. I wouldn't expect you to know that."

"I just think . . ." said Tugs.

"And that's your problem right there, young lady," snapped Mrs. Dostal. "You think too much, when you should be inside helping your mother or dragging that scruffy little cousin of yours somewhere or another, preferably to his own house. Now, I've got real work to do here. Run along and leave adult matters to adults."

"We don't have a lake for sailing," Tugs said as she turned and tromped up her own porch steps.

Ante Up

Tugs shrugged into yesterday's clothes, which still lay in a heap on the floor, slipped past Granny, who was writing a letter at the kitchen table, and collected five pennies from her mother on her way out the door.

Wednesday mornings were Granddaddy Ike's checkers mornings, and in the summer, Tugs was in charge of walking him from his house to Al and Irene's Luncheonette to make sure that (1) he didn't wander off to City Hall or the Baptist church, and (2) he didn't gamble away anything valuable. The importance of the task made Tugs proud.

Granddaddy Ike lived in a tiny cottage next to Ned's, between Tugs's house and downtown. He was older than spit and had been a drummer boy in the Civil War. This afforded him a bit of notoriety around town. His house smelled of sweet pipe tobacco and was cluttered with his collections. He took his meals with Aunt Mina, Uncle Wilson, Ned, and Gladdy, but didn't like them interfering in his day otherwise.

"My savior!" Granddaddy trumpeted when Tugs let herself in the door. "Quick! Let's escape before Mina catches us!" Tugs played along, finding one of Granddaddy's walking sticks and his cap and whispering conspiratorially as she helped him down the sidewalk. The trick today was avoiding Ned. She still hadn't told him she wanted to race with Aggie, and while she hadn't actually said to Aggie that she would race with her, she was sure Aggie assumed it after their Monday practice.

"What are you playing for today?" she

asked, steering him past Ned's house as quickly as she could.

Granddaddy stopped and reached into his pocket.

"Looky at this," he said proudly, holding out a kitchen spoon. "Silver! I slipped it in my pocket after dinner last night. Mina will never notice."

Tugs took the spoon and examined it appreciatively as she got Granddaddy walking again. "Did you ever play the spoons as instruments, with two together?" she asked. That got Granddaddy talking about the old days. He didn't notice when Tugs slipped the spoon in her own pocket so she could give it back to Aunt Mina. She always came prepared with something to substitute if necessary. Like today's pennies.

". . . and that was the end of George," Granddaddy was saying. "Which reminds me, Mina better be pressing my uniform for the All Join In Parade tomorrow."

Tomorrow. Independence Day. Tugs groaned. Maybe it would rain. She looked up at the sky hopefully, but it was frustratingly blue, only a wisp of a cloud floating by.

They turned on Main to see Mayor Corbett standing outside Al and Irene's, carrying on an animated conversation with Harvey Moore.

"Are you any relation to boxing great Gentleman Jim Corbett, Mayor? Should I be ready to duck?"

"Mr. Mayor!" Granddaddy interrupted. "What do you got to say about that upstart come to town to churn out a newspaper? Are you going to give your approval? It's about time we got our own news, I say. The people and places of our own streets and businesses. And our own take on the rest of the country. And pictures. Do you think the *Cedar Rapids Tribune* will cover the dignitaries in tomorrow's parade? No, siree. No, sir. Pits, I say. Pits on Cedar Rapids and their big-wheel attitudes. Pits on Iowa City and their swanky university. And what about the carryings on of our own mayor? Never know what kind of rubbish those yahoos are trying to feed us, I say."

"Mr. Button," Mayor Corbett interrupted. "This is . . ." But Granddaddy wasn't finished.

"It's a free country now, isn't it, Mayor? A fellow doesn't need your approval to start a newspaper, does he? I hear he's a little short of cash, though."

Harvey stuck out his hand and pumped Granddaddy's free one.

"Harvey Moore, pleased to meet you. I am that young upstart, Mr. Button, and you are absolutely right on all fronts. News, right here from Goodhue and the nation. I can tell you are a businessman, Mr. Button, astute as you are about money."

Granddaddy Ike hooked a thumb through his suspender and stood up taller.

"Why, I don't mind telling you . . ."

But Harvey interrupted and continued his flattery of Granddaddy, weaving in his tale of investment opportunity.

Tugs turned away. Harvey Moore reminded her of the balloons at Aggie's party. They grew bigger and bigger as you blew into them, but the minute you let go of the end, the air whooshed out and the balloon wafted away. She wondered when the air would fizzle out of Harvey Moore.

Tugs stopped listening and skimmed the publicity notice for this year's Independence Day picnic posted on Al and Irene's window, looking for announcement of the penny raffle prize.

A Button had never won anything in the penny raffle, but then a Button had never bought a raffle ticket either. It's rigged, they said. Waste of a coin.

Tugs stared at the poster.

She read it quickly, then again.

"It works like a Kodak."

Independence Day Picnic Raffle for A

BROWNIE CAMERA

Pepper's Portraits and Photography is pleased to raffle THREE Brownie Cameras, Brand-New In the Box with One Roll of Film. Come to Pepper's for all your photography and portraiture needs.

BUY YOUR TICKETS NOW!

Purchase your tickets at Ward's Ben Franklin
or Pepper's Portraits and Photography.
The more you buy, the more likely you are to win.

There was a picture of a boy holding a small box in front of his chest, looking down into it with a grin, taking a photo of two girls in frilly dresses.

Tugs reached in her pocket and felt the five pennies her mother had given her for Granddaddy Ike. She rubbed her fingers around their smooth warmth. A camera. She read it again.

Going into Ward's Ben Franklin was out, but she hadn't worn out her welcome at Pepper's, as far as she knew. It was the last day to buy tickets. Tugs turned back to Granddaddy, who was winding up with Harvey Moore and the mayor, and led him inside, where Mr. Jackson and Mr. Everett were waiting.

"Thought you bought the farm!" said Mr. Jackson.

"Thought you'd caught the bus!" said Mr. Everett.

"I got more kick in me than either of

you two geezers," retorted Granddaddy Ike. "What are we playing for?"

He settled into a chair and looked back at Tugs. "Where's the goods?" he asked. "I got to put in."

Tugs hesitated. She could just give him the spoon and take the five pennies to Pepper's. Mr. Jackson and Mr. Everett were used to his odd antes. They'd been known to put in buttons and bow ties and even once a locket of hair from Mr. Everett's horse's tail.

"Luckier than a rabbit's foot, that," he'd said. Granddaddy Ike had wanted to win that horsehair like anything, but Mr. Jackson had taken home the horsehair and a set of Granddaddy's false teeth that day. Granddaddy won back his teeth, but the horsehair never came back to the table.

Today it was toothpicks (Mr. Everett) and tiny tin soldiers (Mr. Jackson). Granddaddy would love to get his hands on those tiny tin soldiers, Tugs was certain. He'd never get them with a spoon. She pulled all five pennies from her pocket and laid them on the table.

Granddaddy flashed his loose teeth around the table. He sat up tall and set up the red chips proudly. "All right, boys, who thinks they can take the loot?"

Tugs watched them get started, then slipped out the door. They'd be busy for an hour if she was lucky.

Just the Ticket

Tugs stepped around Harvey Moore, who had cornered Al outside his luncheonette. She walked down to Pepper's and stood in front of the window. There was a display of the newest Brownie cameras and a poster with an image of a girl about her age taking a picture of a squirrel running up a tree. Tugs scoffed. If she had a camera, she'd certainly photograph something more interesting than a squirrel.

She tried the door, but it was locked. She cupped her hands around her face and pressed her nose against the glass. The store was empty, save for the dozens of camera eyes gazing around the shop.

"Now you've gone and smudged my window!"

Tugs turned. Mr. Pepper had pulled up to the curb and was trying to get an unwieldy box out of his Ford.

"I was . . . the door was . . ." she started, but Mr. Pepper interrupted.

"Never mind. Grab the keys off the front seat, will you? Unlock the door and hold it open for me." Tugs did as she was told and stood holding the door while Mr. Pepper wrestled the box into the store.

"Now, take this rag and go wipe your nose juice off the window."

"I . . ." she started, but Mr. Pepper was already rooting through a drawer and muttering to himself about scissors and numbskulls and the dearth of good help in this country.

Tugs scrubbed at the window of the front door. She couldn't see any smudges, but she wiped anyhow. When she had wiped the outside of the door, she came inside and wiped the inside, too, for good measure.

"Help me out here, would you?" barked Mr. Pepper. He was pulling smaller boxes out of the large box.

"Line these up on the counter as I hand them to you. We have to count them and sort them into types. Have to make sure the distributor didn't short me. These are the most popular items Kodak makes right now, and I'm just a little store in the middle of Nowheresville, Iowa, and even though the people of small-town America deserve cameras as much as the rest of the world, the little guy often gets overlooked. Don't you forget that, young lady."

"I won't forget," said Tugs, lining the boxes up as neatly as she could. Tall as she was and being a girl, she'd never be the little guy. "Did you hear about the newspaper starting up?" Tugs asked.

"Oh, sure. Now, that's what I'm talking about. There's a man with vision. Foresight. In fact, he was in here yesterday, and I don't mind telling you, he asked me to be his photographic consultant. Says he'll buy a camera from this very shop when the paper gets under way. Not going to send away to Chicago, to some fancy schmancy store. No. That man knows quality when he sees it. I paid him for six months of advertising in advance. Might have to hire someone on, all the business I'm going to get in here."

"You gave him money already?" said Tugs. "But there's no paper yet."

"Humph. I can't expect you to know how business works. Of course I gave him money in advance. How else is he going to get the paper up and running? Now, pay attention to what you're doing, young lady."

Tugs handled the boxes gingerly, wishing she were taking one home with her.

The count came out just as the invoice directed, which made Mr. Pepper pleased at last.

"Well," he said, leaning against the counter. "There we go, then." He sighed heavily and nearly smiled at Tugs. "I guess you've been quite a help." He reached under the counter and brought out a string of five raffle tickets. "Got a few left. Here you go. For your efforts. Write your name on the back and drop them in that box at the end of the counter. Maybe you'll get lucky."

"Really?" Tugs grinned. "Swell. I mean, great. I mean, thanks, and where's a pencil?" Mr. Pepper handed her a pencil and she got busy printing her name as clearly as possible.

"Hurry up, then. You're not writing a novel there."

"I'm putting my whole name on. Just in case," she said.

Mr. Pepper craned his neck to see her name.

"I shouldn't think there would be too many Tugs Buttons that weren't you," he said.

"Never know," she said as she finished the last ticket and dropped it in the box. She looked into the narrow slot. "Awful lot of tickets in there."

"Each one has as good a chance as any

other," said Mr. Pepper. "Kid, adult, never can tell."

"Who picks the winners?"

"The president of the art guild. This year that's me."

Tugs started toward the door, then turned back.

"Can I look into one?" she asked.

"Well, sure, then. I guess that wouldn't hurt."

Mr. Pepper pulled a Brownie from the display case and handed it to her. "Now, hold it down. . . . Yes, that's it."

The camera had a pleasing weight in her hands as she studied the small image of Mr. Pepper in the box.

"Click," she said, then handed it back. "It's the best raffle prize ever, if you ask me." Tugs took one more long look at the case of cameras, then remembered Granddaddy and ran out the door, counting as she ran, *one, two, one, two.*

Independence Day

Burglars could have a fine day of it in Goodhue on the Fourth of July, with the whole
population emptied into the town park,
like so many checkers swept off a winning
board. But the unscrupulous elements typi-
cally found more business in the heart of
the celebration, the occasional out-of-town
pickpocket making suspects of everyone's
visiting cousin or uncle.

After the All Join In Parade, eating was
the primary occupation, with families and
neighbors joining together to make huge
smorgasbord picnics and kids roaming from
one blanket to the next to find the best fare.

This year the Buttons got to the park late and had to squeeze themselves between the Floyds and the Novaks on the outer edge, nearly on top of the railroad tracks. There were advantages to this spot—they'd feel the ground rumble if a train were approaching, and the rise of the hill gave them a good view of the goings-on.

Tugs pushed her potato salad around her plate with her fork. Her stomach was tight with dread. She had to tell Ned, but not here, with their mothers listening.

Tugs saw a Panama bob through the crowd, pausing for a minute here, a minute there, and covering the grounds like a bee collecting nectar from a field of daffodils.

"Come on, Ned," Tugs said. She set her plate on the ground, where the Floyds' three-legged dog, Lulu, could clean it for her.

"Where are we going?" asked Ned, jogging to keep up with her. "I don't want to get worn out before the race."

"We're going to see what Harvey Moore is up to."

"Why?"

"We just are."

"But the race is going to start soon."

"Don't worry."

As they drew up behind Harvey, Tugs slowed and held out her arm to stop Ned.

"Let's just follow him for a little ways."

"But . . ." said Ned.

"Shhh."

Harvey was unaware of his shadows. He and the Perkins were engrossed in conversation.

"And all we need to bring this venture to Goodhue is one hundred prepaid annual subscribers and thirty advertising commitments. I have a line on a used press that the seller will part with for a modest down payment and throw in the paper to boot. Prominent on the front page of the first issue will be the names of each of the founding subscribers." Harvey painted a swath in the air with his hand.

"Franklin and Evelyn Perkins," he said grandly. "Imagine it. Bold print. Fourteen-point sans serif type. In fact, if you are one of the first twenty-five subscribers to the *Goodhue Progress,* I could make that eighteen-point and put your name at the top of the list."

Mrs. Perkins clapped her hands. "Franklin!" she exclaimed. "Fancy what Wilma will say when she sees our name in the paper. I always told her I'd be somebody, and she didn't believe me. Thinks she's so high-class, living over there in Iowa City. Imagine. A daily. Right here in Goodhue. With our names on it."

"Well, Mother," said Mr. Perkins. Even though their children were grown, he still called his wife Mother. "I don't know that we've got enough news for a daily, but I suppose a few dollars to impress Wilma . . . I don't have that much cash on me at the moment, as you can imagine, but I could bring it . . ."

"No, no," said Harvey. "I'll come to you. Just write your address here next to your commitment signature, and if you have any cash for down payment . . ."

"Progress," said Mr. Perkins as he wrote. "Now, that's a name." He dug in his pocket and handed Harvey a bill.

"Thank you, Mr. Perkins. Mrs. Perkins," said Harvey. "You're investing in Goodhue. You're investing in progress." He shook both their hands before moving on.

"See?" whispered Ned. "Mr. Moore is for progress. And he said he'd help me with catching and tossing. So leave him alone."

"I guess," said Tugs. "It's just that progress seems to cost an awful lot."

Tugs saw Aggie just then and turned to Ned.

"Meet me back at the blanket, OK? I have something to do."

Ned wove his way back to the Buttons as Tugs dodged toddlers and mothers and found her way to Aggie.

"Tugs!" cried Aggie. "I've been look-ing all over for you. It's nearly time for the three-legged."

"I haven't told Ned yet," Tugs confessed.

"You haven't?"

"I tried, but . . ."

"Come on, then," said Aggie briskly. "Let's find him a partner." Aggie dragged Tugs by the arm over to the sprawl of the Stump gathering, under the center oak with the low-hanging branches. A jumble of squat Stump children tumbled from the tree and landed in a pile.

"Which one of you is in Ned Button's grade?" Aggie demanded.

"Ralph," said Tugs, marveling at Aggie's ability to unravel a knot, while Tugs herself had spent days letting this dilemma pick at her.

Ralph popped up from the bottom of the pile.

"Who wants to know?"

"You're racing the three-legged with

Ned," said Aggie. "Come on, it's nearly time." Aggie's tone was commanding, and despite himself, Ralph Stump followed the girls.

"I ask Ned every year and he always says he has a partner," whined Ralph. "He's not going to want to race with me."

"Sure he wants to race with you," said Tugs, catching Aggie's enthusiasm. "He just thinks you're too fast and he wouldn't have a chance to keep up with you. Ask him again."

"But—" Ralph panted, trying to keep up with the long-legged girls, but they had sprinted away and were already at the blanket, prepping Ned.

"Ned, Ralph Stump really wants to race with you," Aggie said. "So I said I'd race with Tugs."

Ned stared. Aggie Millhouse knew his name. Aggie Millhouse was talking to him. He grinned.

"W-w-what?" he stammered.

Tugs rolled her eyes. "Aggie said she'd race with me so you can race with Ralph."

Ralph caught up then. He was breathing too hard to talk and just raised his hand to Ned before flopping on the ground.

They heard Mr. Floyd's trumpet blast announcing the start of the afternoon's events.

Aggie grabbed Ralph's arm and pulled him up. "Do you two want to miss the race altogether?"

The boys didn't have a chance to consider their new partnership. They set off after the girls.

Ribbons

Aggie and Tugs elbowed their way to the coveted outside edge of the start line, where they would be less likely to be bumped off course. Ned and Ralph nudged their way in next to Aggie and Tugs. The high-school track team was in charge of organizing the races for the younger children. The middle Floyd girl walked down the line with a box of fabric strips for tying legs together, while Lester Ward made sure that no one put so much as a toe on the field before the whistle was blown.

"On your mark!" called Lester, but there was a hubbub at the line when three teams on the other end fell onto the field. The track team hurried to stand them upright and move them behind the start line, but then toward the middle of the line, another team went sprawling onto the field.

Tugs craned her neck to see what was going on. It was the Rowdies, slipping behind the runners, knocking random pairs to the ground. G.O. was with them. Teams were stepping out of formation, turning to see if they were going to be next.

"Get set!" Lester called.

G.O. spotted Tugs just then and started toward her.

"Just keep your head down and count," Aggie urged. "Inside leg first."

"Go!" Lester hollered as the whistle blared.

"One!" called Aggie and Tugs together. They launched their inside feet across the start line just as the Rowdies melted back into the crowd, leaving G.O. standing in the field of runners. The rest of the teams, startled into starting before they were ready, stumbled, fell, got up, tried again, bumped into one another, jostled, and generally clumped along. G.O. got knocked down in the fray. Tugs and Aggie kept their heads down and simply walked steadily, chanting *one, two, one, two,* crossing the line still standing.

"We won!" Aggie cried, grabbing Tugs in a hug.

"We did?" said Tugs. She looked around. Sure enough, they were standing at the bandstand. The Floyd girl thrust blue ribbons into their hands before hurrying off to help the other teams as they straggled in.

Tugs rubbed the smooth surface of her ribbon between her fingers, marveling at the royalness of the blue, as Aggie untied their legs.

Tugs's reverie was interrupted by G.O. shouting, "Let me go! I didn't do nothing." Lester Ward had collared him and was dragging him away.

"Look," said Aggie. "He got G.O."

Feeling brave and magnanimous with a ribbon in her hand, Tugs shouted, "Let him go, Lester Ward! It was the Rowdies, not G.O.!"

Lester looked back sharply to see who was hollering at him, and G.O. slipped out of his grip and ran away.

"Let's get out of here!" Aggie hissed, grabbing Tugs's arm. They darted away, laughing at their own bravery and stupidity.

Then they heard Mr. Floyd's trumpet. People were drifting toward the bandstand.

"Come on," said Aggie.

The sight of Harvey Moore standing next to the mayor on the podium dampened Tugs's spirit. Harvey Moore was everywhere. There was a red-white-and-blue ribbon tied around his hat, and aside from the mayor and Mr. Millhouse, he was the only man wearing a suit to the Independence Day picnic.

"Let's watch from back here," said Tugs. Could she confess her suspicions about

Harvey Moore to Aggie? Would Aggie believe her? She glanced over at Aggie.

"Aggie, I got to tell you something important," she started, but she was interrupted by Harvey Moore himself, who pulled Mayor Corbett's megaphone from his hand and bellowed, "Good afternoon!"

The crowd did not simmer down.

Harvey tried again, drawing out his words like a caller at the track. "Gooood afternoon, Goooodhue! How about this day?"

A few people clapped.

"That's the man from Chicago," Tugs heard a woman behind her say.

"I wonder if there's a Mrs. Chicago," said another. "Or if he'd like one."

"I heard he's the nephew of the governor," the first woman said.

"Really? I heard he is a railroad baron, come to invest in Goodhue."

"Lovely people of Goodhue!" Harvey continued, undaunted by the hubbub. "Your fine mayor here has asked me to say a few words before the announcement of the patriotic essay awards." The crowd began to settle.

"Look at this crowd. *This* is patriotism, people. An entire town gathered to celebrate the birth of our nation. And what a nation it is. Goodhue represents the best of what makes this country great. Why, a virtual stranger can enter this place and find unmatched hospitality—thank you to the Dostals for taking me in, by the by—hello out there, Dostals!" Harvey waved in the general direction of the Dostals' blanket. There was a smattering of applause.

"Yes, a fellow can come to this town with an idea for progress. An idea that will give your dear children a chance at living in a town of substance. A wild idea? Maybe. A bold idea? Probably. An idea that citizens of other towns have not been brave enough to believe in? Absolutely.

"Did the people of this town, the people of Goodhue, Iowa, snuff that idea out? No!

The people of this town are opening their minds and pocketbooks and saying yes to progress.

"The Dostals said yes to progress. The Perkinses said yes to progress. The esteemed William Millhouse the Third said yes to progress. The only question that remains is this." Harvey paused. The crowd went silent, hanging on his every word.

"The question remains: will *you* say yes to progress?" Harvey let a long beat go by as the crowd considered his question.

"What is progress, you ask? Bear with me a moment. One of Goodhue's own sons, Lester Ward, is leaving the nest soon. Not only is Lester going to be an Iowa Hawkeye; he's going to be an Iowa Hawkeye *football* player." The crowd cheered. Harvey raised his hand.

"Now, how will you get news of Lester's glory? His parents, sure. Some of you will go to the games, no doubt. Others will listen on the radio. But what about the story of the game? The story that lists the name of one of your own in its pages? The one you can snip out and paste in a scrapbook? Will they feed you that story in the *Cedar Rapids Tribune*? No, sir. I am here, ladies and gentlemen, to bring the newspaper back to Goodhue. The *Goodhue Progress*. With your help, we can bring progress to Goodhue. Find me after the announcements here, and put your down payment on progress.

"Now, on to the business at hand! Mayor, the list of essay winners, please."

"Progress?" said the woman behind Tugs. "I thought we were going to get a bowling alley."

"That's what I heard," said a man next to her.

"It's a newspaper," said Aggie, turning to the people behind them. "Really. We're going to have a daily newspaper."

"Oh!" said the man.

"Well, I never," said the woman.

". . . and the blue-ribbon essay for age

thirteen and older . . ." Harvey Moore called, "goes to Florence Floyd! Where's Florence? Come up here, Florence, and inspire us with your words!"

"Come on," said the woman behind Tugs. "Let's try to intercept Mr. Moore when he comes down the steps."

As Florence read in her high fluted voice, Aggie turned back to Tugs.

"What was the important thing you wanted to tell me?"

Tugs wavered. Maybe she was just imagining things. Maybe Harvey really was going to start a newspaper.

"Nothing," she said. She held up her ribbon. "We won the three-legged, Aggie."

"Did you see the look on Burton Ward's face when he came in behind us?" said Aggie. "That was worth the price of admission."

Tugs was suddenly hungry, and she pulled Aggie toward the Button blanket.

But then they heard ". . . Button" over the megaphone and turned around.

"Tugs, Tugs Button. Is Tugs Button here?" bellowed Harvey Moore. "Well, sorry to disappoint you, folks, but it appears our eight-to-twelve division winner is not present. Let's go on. . . ."

"Tugs!" gasped Aggie. "You won the essay contest! Come on!"

Aggie dashed off, but Tugs's feet were stuck. There must be some mistake.

Then she heard Aggie's voice ring out. Aggie Millhouse was standing on the bandstand, holding the megaphone and beckoning her to come up for her ribbon. But it was too much for Tugs. She ducked behind the nearest tree and listened as Aggie accepted her ribbon for her and read her essay aloud. Her hunger vanished and was replaced with a mix of fear and elation. She heard her own words echoing over the crowd and wondered if she'd really written them. Her face burned with the horror of it, all those people hearing her thoughts.

She peeked out. Aggie was skipping

down the steps and running back to Tugs, with Tugs's second blue ribbon held high as she ran.

"Here!" Aggie said. "I've never won two blue ribbons, Tugs. Your essay was really good."

Tugs and Aggie linked arms and walked back to the Buttons' blanket, where such a commotion had occurred over Grand-daddy's betting on the horseshoe contest that the adults had missed the goings-on at the field and bandstand. Ned was sitting alone behind the Button blanket, leaning against the tracks.

Mother Button stood up when Tugs introduced her to Aggie.

"Oh, heavens, a Millhouse at our blanket and we're fresh out of"— she looked around at the crumbs and empty dishes —"everything."

"That's OK," said Aggie. "I have to check in with my family. Want to come, Tugs?"

Tugs looked at Ned, then back at Aggie.

"I'll catch up with you later," she said.

She watched Aggie disappear behind a group of Floyds returning to their blanket, then sat down next to Ned.

"Can I see?" Ned asked, holding out his hand.

"Sure," said Tugs, and handed him her ribbons.

"They're shiny," he said.

"You can hold them," said Tugs. She felt full-up satisfied.

Click

After a couple of lazy hours, Aunt Mina heaved herself off the ground and bustled about, packing baskets and folding blankets.

"Let's get picking up here, people. They've got the tug-a-war going on down there, and next thing you know, they'll be announcing the raffle. If we don't leave now, we'll get caught in the going-home rush. I, for one, am ready to get home to my own four walls."

The Buttons started the long trek through the park. Tugs lagged behind, hoping to hear at least who did win the raffle. Had she spelled her name right? Had Mr. Pepper taken her free tickets out so that only paying tickets would be in the box? She fingered her ribbons proudly. Ribbons should be enough. But . . .

Then the band blared and Granddaddy Ike stopped to listen. He was near the front of the Button line, so they all had to stop. The moment the band was finished with its fanfare, Mr. Pepper stood up.

"As the president of the garden club and the art guild, and as proprietor of your hometown photography store—come to Pepper's for all your photography needs—I am proud to draw names for this year's raffle prizes—three Kodak Brownie cameras!" He reached his hand into the hat Harvey Moore had lent him for this purpose and drew out a name.

"Mrs. Perkins!" he called. There was applause and a squeal from Mrs. Perkins as she made her way to the stage.

"Orion Ortner!" Another smattering of applause as the town butcher walked to the stage.

"And last but not least, Tugs Button!"

Tugs stood, dumbfounded.

"Tugs Button!" Mr. Pepper said again, and Tugs ran up to the stage.

Mr. Pepper handed her a smart little box, just like the ones she'd unpacked at his store. She opened the cover and lifted out the camera.

"Green!" she said triumphantly. She dropped the box and manual on the step and held the camera out to Mr. Pepper. "Now what?"

Mr. Pepper laughed. "No reading the manual for you, Miss Button?" He opened her camera and wound film into the empty spool while Tugs hopped from foot to foot, looking around to see who was noticing that this was her camera Mr. Pepper was readying.

"Granddaddy Ike! Over here!" she hollered.

"Now, pay attention, Miss Button, so you can do this yourself next time," Mr. Pepper said.

"*Miss Button!* Ha, ha, ha!" Tugs snorted. She could sooner fly to the moon than concentrate on Mr. Pepper's dainty fingers. He'd called her Miss Button! She won the Kodak raffle! The camera was green! Her favorite color! The color of early wheat, and the sky before a summer storm, and moss on stones by the river, and . . . !

"Here you are," said Mr. Pepper, handing the camera back to Tugs. "Six pictures to a roll, so look and think before you snap. Don't open the back before the roll is wound clear through. And come to Pepper's to buy more film."

Tugs held the camera out in front of her, like a crystal egg. It was so beautiful. Her hands were suddenly slick, and she was afraid she'd drop it. Mr. Pepper laughed.

"This here is the new aluminum model. You aren't going to hurt it, girly. Now, go have . . ."

But Tugs saw the Millhouses standing near the Buttons just then and left Mr.

Pepper at a gallop, forgetting the box and to shout a thank-you over her shoulder.

"Well, I'll be a chicken's gizzard," said her mother.

"Better take that girl to the track," said her father.

"Are you sure she's one of us?" asked Granddaddy Ike.

"Sure, I'm sure," said Tugs. "I got the chompers, don't I?"

There was no denying it. Tugs had the teeth of a Button—square, wide, and protruding. For as long as anyone could remember, Button children had been teased about their maws. It was one root of their misfortune, the Buttons believed. While other parents sent their children off to school with a kiss and told them to do their best, the Buttons just said, "Don't get hit by the tater truck." Which would be nonsense to any other family, but Leonard Button, one of the Swisher Buttons, had indeed looked the wrong way when crossing Main Street some years ago. While he had survived, he hadn't eaten a potato, mashed or otherwise, since.

It didn't seem sporting to document failure, so Buttons didn't own cameras, yet here was Tugs with a fetching green leatherette Kodak No. 2 Brownie F model, loaded with film to boot.

"Hold these ribbons, Aggie," Tugs commanded. She aimed her Brownie and tried to capture her winnings on film. But Mrs. Millhouse yoo-hooed just then, and Tugs snapped the shutter right as Aggie spun around.

"Dagnabit!" said Tugs.

"Tugs Button — such language!" gasped Mrs. Millhouse, pulling Aggie away. "Come on, sweetness."

"My ribbons, Aggie!" Tugs yelled. Turning to give them back, Aggie tripped over little Winslow Ward, and they both went sprawling in the dirt.

"Figures," Burton Ward said to Tugs as

he picked up his wailing brother. "You're such a Button."

"Sorry!" Aggie called as she was hustled away by her mother. Tugs picked up her trampled ribbons and tucked them in the pocket of her overalls.

"See you next week?" she hollered.

"Going to camp!" Aggie called as she was eclipsed by Harvey Moore and the dispersing crowd. Tugs clicked the shutter again.

Tugs looked down through her camera's viewfinder and pivoted slowly all the way around and down and up. It was like watching a movie, seeing the bandstand, the bakery, the soft evening sky go by in that tiny frame. These were the same ordinary sights she'd been seeing her whole life, but suddenly they were sharp and beautiful, like little jewels collected in a box. To think—only this morning she'd been an ordinary twelve-year-old girl with snarly hair, gangly limbs, and a propensity for calamity, and now, just hours later, here she stood, Tugs Button: ribbon winner, Kodak owner.

She held the camera at arm's length, smiled into the eye of its lens, and pressed the exposure lever. Then she turned the winding key until a little number four appeared in the red window on the back.

"Let me see." Luther Tingvold towered over Tugs, holding out his hand.

"Um," said Tugs, clutching her camera close. Luther was the leader of the Rowdies.

"I want to see!" hollered Walter Williams, stepping in front of Luther.

"Take our picture, Tugs!" said Finn and Frankie Chacey, making ape faces while trying to shove Walter out of the way.

"Trade you my pocketknife for it," growled Bess McCrea, the toughest girl in town.

Tugs didn't know whether to be flattered or afraid. No Rowdy had ever said hello to her, much less wanted something she had. Their attention both thrilled and frightened her. She had to do something clever now, say something clever.

"It's green," she blurted out.

Finn and Frankie guffawed. Bess shook her head in disgust. Luther shrugged and turned away.

"Last one to the fire hydrant's a horse's patoot!" called Walter, and they all took off running.

Tugs aimed her Brownie after them and pushed the lever. She adored the satisfying *click* it made.

"Now, don't go getting a swell head," said Father Button as he took Tugs's elbow and led her back to the car. "And take your eyes outa those clouds. We got a big day tomorrow — family reunion."

At home Tugs cleared a spot on her dresser for her camera and tied her ribbons to the drawer pulls so she would see them first thing when she woke.

Such a Button

This July Fourth fortune was good for Tugs, but over to Elmer Button's farm the next day, where for the last umpteen years the family had been gathering to share their annual midsummer woes, the fizz wasn't out of their Cokes before the other Buttons started grumbling. Twenty-seven Buttons took shelter under a wide oak as drizzle turned the back forty to mud and mosquitoes buzzed in the hot, still air.

"I understand Tugs was paired with the sixth grade's top athlete in that race," snapped Aunt Mina. "My Ned could have won if he hadn't been strapped with that shrimp Ralph Stump."

Cousin Gladdy was indignant. "I heard Mrs. Potter telling Mrs. Winthrop that *my* essay was best, and I'm only eight," she said. "I bet it was rigged."

"She's made a pact with the devil," screeched Grandmother Adeline. "No one's ever won a dang thing in this family. Who does she think she is, one of the Floyd girls?"

"Aw, Granny," said Tugs, patting Granny's stooped shoulder. "I've got two left feet like everyone else in this family. Come on, I'll take your picture."

"Humph," said Granny, and poked Tugs with her cane. "Get away from me, devil child."

Tugs swatted the cane away and held the Brownie in front of her belly. She saw through the viewfinder a square of Granny coming closer. "Wait, Granny," Tugs said. "Just smile." She saw Granny's scowling face, then Granny's bony hand, then with a yank, Granny grabbed the camera from Tugs and held it to her own chest, letting her cane fall to the ground.

"I said. I do not. Want my image taken."

"Hey!" Tugs protested, and reached for the camera in Granny's clutches. Granny teetered, then toppled over, and the Brownie flew out of her hands. Aunt Mina, rushing to help Granny, didn't see the camera and tramped on it with her sturdy shoes. The softened ground gave a bit, but not enough to keep it intact under the weight of Aunt Mina.

Aunt Mina lifted her foot and looked at the dented cube.

"Really!" she said, shaking her finger at Tugs. "Cameras are little glass boxes. You can't go *dropping* them, Tugs. What do you expect?"

Tears welled immediately in Tugs's eyes. She wiped her hand across her face.

"But I . . ." Tugs started, but by then Granny had set up a wail.

"Old lady on the ground here, people! Oh, me! I might be broken!"

Granny was a tiny bit of a woman, and Ned was able to lift her to her feet. He handed Granny her cane and stepped back, in case she decided to poke him, too.

As Tugs bent down to pick up her camera, she overheard one of the Swisher Buttons say, "That'll teach her to show everyone up. I mean, two blue ribbons *and* a Kodak? Serves her right."

Something snapped in Tugs then. Why shouldn't she have a brand-new camera? Why shouldn't she be the lucky one? She was tired of being a Button. Tired of being the one who comes up short, loses the ball for the team, gets blamed for everything. She stood and faced her grumbling kin.

"Would all you people just . . . CLAP your TRAPS!"

There was a collective gasp and then a stunned silence. Aunt Mina put her hands over Gladdy's ears. Tugs had surprised herself, too. But she stood tall and spoke into the hush.

"You ought to be ashamed of yourselves. All you do is complain, every one of you."

"What kind of parents are you?" Granny hollered to no one in particular. "Shut her up, will you?"

"Granny!" Aunt Mina exclaimed, and clamped her hand over Granny's mouth.

Tugs ignored them. "Burton was wrong. I am *not* such a Button. I am lucky. And I'm going to go on being lucky. You just watch."

The Buttons gaped at Tugs as if she'd declared herself Swedish, or musical, two of life's many impossibilities.

"Hear, hear!" exclaimed Granddaddy Ike, waving his cap while the rest of the Buttons resumed their squawking.

"Well, now," said Father Button. "Well. There's our girl. Well." He put his arm around Tugs's shoulder and they walked out from under the tree. "Come on, Corrine," he said to Mother Button. "Let's go home now. Mina, you can drop Granny off later."

"What did she say?" demanded Granny. "*Plucky*? She's not a plucky Button. I'm pluckier than the whole lot of you nincompoops. Why, I've been a widow since aught seven, and . . ."

"Bring that girl back here to apologize," interrupted Aunt Mina. "Shoving and sassing and foul language cannot be tolerated!" But Tugs and her parents trod on.

Tugs was rolling down her window when Ned ran up.

"Me, too!" he whispered into the car. "Help me be lucky, too!" Then he turned and said, so that everyone else could hear, "And don't you ever mess with our Granny again!"

Tugs sank into the backseat, her Brownie on her lap. The silver exposure lever was stuck. The tiny glass viewfinder was cracked. The side was dented. But remarkably, when she held it up to the window, she could see Buttons large and small, all split and angled like a kaleidoscope.

"Click," Tugs said. There was her family. Then the car lurched forward and she saw fractured fields of corn fly by. She angled her Kodak upward and saw the weight of the fractured clouds. A dismembered crow crossed the frame.

The Buttons bumped along the muddy rutted road, windows down to lure a breeze. Tugs waited for reprimand, but none came. She supposed it wasn't the best luck to begin her lucky life by yelling at her elders. But it was done, and despite the ache her damaged camera produced, she felt surprisingly free and light. Lucky. She was lucky. Her heart sat high in her chest, and she would have sung a tune if she could have thought of a tune to sing. Buttons were not singers.

Come to think of it, there were a lot of things the Buttons weren't. Buttons weren't dancers. They weren't athletes or readers or jokesters or artists. They weren't good students or good listeners or standout citizens. The only time a Button had made the *Goodhue Gazette,* back when there was a *Goodhue Gazette,* was when Granddaddy Ike accidentally set the town hall on fire with a cigarette, when he nodded off in the lobby next to a full trash can. Not much chance of Buttons appearing in the new *Goodhue Progress,* either.

Just as quickly as it came, Tugs's euphoria evaporated. Was she just a Button, as Burton said? She looked at her mother's long neck, her father's unruly hair, and recognized herself as their miniature. But while she couldn't name it, Tugs had felt a sense of possibility today as she made that small speech, and there had to be a way to get that feeling back.

Up to the Task

It was while lying atop the covers the next morning, mulling over Aunt Mina's admonishment that cameras were little glass boxes, that Tugs remembered what she'd left at the park on the Fourth of July: the Kodak box and the manual with it. If she had the manual, maybe she could fix her camera.

Tugs played over the scene again in her mind. *The new aluminum model,* Mr. Pepper had said. Aunt Mina was wrong. Cameras were not little glass boxes. And there was an instruction manual somewhere to guide her.

Tugs smoothed out her bedspread and laid her Brownie on it. She got a butter knife from the kitchen drawer and pried the exposure lever back to its correct position. She tried turning the winding key, but the dented side was stopping things up. It wasn't split open, though. So it wasn't technically *broken,* and that was lucky. Her fingers itched to open the back and see what was inside, but she remembered Mr. Pepper's words and resisted.

How did the picture making happen? The viewing window was a problem. Would the cracks show up in photos? Could the Brownie still take photos? Tugs studied the camera's face, running her finger over the ridged eye of the lens opening. Even the lens cover was green, a detail that delighted her. There were two tiny glass windows down in the corner, with a tiny silver nail between them. What were they for?

The front cover must come off. Mr. Pepper hadn't said it wouldn't. She pulled on it cautiously but didn't dare pry too hard. She held the cube of it between her two palms. It was cool to the touch and nearly smooth, the pine green of the surface mottled by thin lighter green lines running in random paths.

Oh, the beauty of it. This little box could capture the world. How had she not known that she needed just this very thing in her life? Just the owning of it made her forget her ornery relatives, her jaggedy grin, the way Bess had turned away from her at the park. She felt important.

Tugs was not generally one to take good care of things. Her clothes lay in a heap on the floor. The doll she'd had since she was six was missing an arm, and its tiny checked dress was torn. When she'd gotten Swisher cousin Nora's hand-me-down bicycle last year, she'd left it on the front porch and it had been stolen in the night.

But the camera would be different, she vowed to herself. Her name had been drawn in that raffle, as if the hand of Luck herself had chosen her—Tugs Esther Button. Tugs imagined Luck as a kindly ancient grandmother, a sweeter version of her own tart wrinkly Granny, but just as feisty in her ability to turn events to her whim. And if Luck wanted her to have a green Kodak No. 2 Brownie F model, Tugs would stand up to the task.

Too bad she'd already mismanaged the box and instruction manual. There was no chance it would still be at the park two days later, what with G.O.'s family and their scavenging obsession. Couldn't drop a Hershey's wrapper without some Lindholm sweeping in to claim it for a wrapper sculpture or some such. They would have been over and through that park quick as a wink, picking up trash and claiming anything left behind. No such thing as a lost and found department in a town inhabited by a clan of finders keepers. And even if they did find the manual, G.O. certainly wouldn't give it to her.

On Display

Tugs had yet to need information that couldn't be found at the library. She could find a camera instruction book there, sure. First thing Monday morning, Tugs scoured the house for *Rootabaga Stories*. She wore her blue ribbons pinned to the front of her overalls and carried her Kodak by its little leather strap.

Miss Lucy was busy with the Thompson twins, sisters who lived together in the little house next to the library and still dressed identically, though they were old ladies. Tugs put her book on the returns shelf and went to the dictionary while she waited.

Lucky, said the dictionary, meant *favored by luck; fortunate; meeting with good success or good fortune.*

Tugs flipped to *fortune.*

Fortune: the arrival of something in a sudden or unexpected manner; chance; accident; luck; destiny.

Destiny: the fixed order of things; invincible necessity; fate.

Fate: predetermined event; destiny; especially, the final lot; doom.

Luck, fortune, destiny, fate, doom. It was a perplexing circle.

"What's the word of the day?" asked Miss Lucy.

"Oh!" said Tugs a little too loudly. "Nothing!" She knocked her camera off the table, scooted off the stool to pick it up, and stood, blushing.

"Well, Tugs Button, would you look at those ribbons. Aren't you the cat's meow?"

said Miss Lucy. Tugs turned redder yet. She tried to think of something clever to say, but could only come up with, "You got a coffee spot on your blouse, Miss Lucy."

"Why, so I do. I must have been in a hurry this morning. Now, tell me about those ribbons."

"Three-legged race. Aggie Millhouse," Tugs said, pointing to the first ribbon. Then she unpinned the second ribbon and handed it to Miss Lucy. "Essay," she said, and her chest filled so fast she was sure the whole of Goodhue could hear the air rush in. She was getting not only the swell head her father warned against, but a swell chest as well. It was impulse, but she wanted Miss Lucy to have that essay ribbon. "Keep it."

Miss Lucy opened her mouth to protest, but then shut it again and held the ribbon aloft, as if inspecting a sweet summer tomato. "I know just what let's do. Come on."

Tugs followed her to the office, where Miss Lucy rummaged for the key to the display case and stuck a pin between her teeth. Just inside the foyer, she unlocked the case and pinned Tugs's ribbon next to a small American flag and a feature on Betsy Ross. Then she plucked a pencil from behind her ear and printed neatly below it, *TUGS BUTTON: PATRIOTIC ESSAY WINNER 1929.*

"There," said Miss Lucy. "Now, bring that essay next time you come in and we'll hang it with the ribbon."

Tugs nodded, but she knew she wouldn't. The ribbon was enough. Probably too much, even. Displaying the essay would certainly be putting on airs.

The door swung open and Burton Ward came in, dragging Winslow by the hand. "Button," he scoffed under his breath as he passed Tugs. Tugs's stomach dropped. She hoped Miss Lucy didn't know about the Ben Franklin incident.

"Button!" mimicked Winslow, not so quietly.

Miss Lucy turned and said loud enough

for the whole library to hear, "Sorry we don't have room to put *all* of your blue ribbons in the case, Tugs." Then she scurried after Winslow, who was randomly pulling books off shelves as he passed, and Tugs slipped out the front door, forgetting entirely about the camera instruction manual.

Three Marys

Tugs was studying the sidewalk so hard as she walked home from the library, trying to avoid stepping on the cracks between the squares, that she nearly walked smack into Ned, who came charging around the corner full speed ahead.

"Ned!" she said.

"Tugs!" he said.

"Huh," said Tugs.

"Yep," said Ned.

"I was at the library," said Tugs.

"I know."

"You do?"

"Granny said."

"Well."

"Why aren't you with Aggie?"

"She's at camp."

They watched Mrs. Perkins chase the Wards' cat out of her petunias.

"I'm on my way home," said Tugs.

"I'll walk with you," said Ned.

"But where were you going?" asked Tugs.

"The library," said Ned.

"Well, I guess I could walk with *you,* then," said Tugs.

"OK," said Ned, scratching a patch of mosquito bites. "I saw Mr. Moore."

"Oh."

"He was in the phone booth outside the Ben Franklin."

"Hmmm."

"The door was open and I sort of overheard him say something strange."

Tugs glanced over at Ned.

"Well?"

"He said Goodhue was ripe, or maybe it was, 'Time is right for picking.' What did he mean?"

"Don't know," said Tugs.

"I thought you were interested in what he is up to."

Tugs shrugged. Her mind was muddled over what had happened at the library. She had a ribbon hanging in the display case, with her name printed right there for everyone who walked into the library to see. It had been exciting in the moment, but now she had doubts.

What if people thought she was showing off? What if she *was* showing off? Would they know Miss Lucy had been the one to put the ribbon in the case, or would they think that a Button such as herself would have picked the lock and stuck the ribbon in there uninvited? Yet if there was one thing Buttons were not, it was criminals. She would never pick a lock.

Her heart beat faster with the indignity of it all, and she brooded as they climbed the library steps.

Tugs followed Ned through the door and

stopped in front of the case. Her stomach clenched. How had she not seen how dirty and wrinkled her ribbon was? It looked like a used ribbon, not the ribbon of a real win-ner. Aggie Millhouse would never display a dirty ribbon.

"Ned!" she whispered as Ned stepped into the library. "What do you need at the library?"

It took Ned a moment to remember.

"You!" he said.

"But I'm right here." Tugs glanced around the library, but no one had noticed them yet, not even Miss Lucy, whose concentration was still completely taken with the Ward boys. "Come on, let's go."

Miss Lucy, in her haste to chase Winslow, had left the display case open. Tugs tucked her camera under one arm, reached into the case, grabbed her ribbon, and ducked out the door, a puzzled Ned trailing behind her.

Back outside, Tugs was suddenly tired.

"Let's watch cars," she said, and flopped down on the bench that sat at the edge of the library yard, facing Main Street.

"Model T," said Ned.

"Olds," said Tugs.

"Whippet!" they said together. There wasn't much traffic, but then there never was in Goodhue.

"That was lucky, anyhow," said Tugs.

"What?" said Ned hopefully.

"The case was still open."

"Oh," said Ned, nodding as if he understood. "Yep, that was lucky."

"I guess I should get home," Tugs said.

"Me too," said Ned.

They were almost to the Perkinses' house when they saw the three Marys roller-skating toward them. Mary Alice, Mary Helen, and Mary Louise were not only best friends; they were also beautiful, with straight hair, straight teeth, and small, plump limbs. Seeing them for the first time since Aggie's party, sailing down the sidewalk, their matching skirts billowing, their laughing faces glowing, it was as if the pages she'd just read in the dictionary, *luck, fortune,* were skimming toward her. Tugs found herself wishing to be a Mary, too.

Tugs waved.

"Hiya, Mary Alice, Mary Helen, Mary Louise!" she hollered.

"Well, if it isn't Tugs Button and her little sidekick," said Mary Alice as the three skated to a neat stop. "Where are you off to, nursery school?"

"My house," said Tugs. She smiled in what she hoped was a carefree summer-afternoon sort of way, then remembered her buckteeth and her cousin next to her. She pulled her top lip down and chewed on her lower lip. The Marys started to go around her.

"Want to come with?" she said. "To my house?" She stepped in front of Ned. "He's not coming." She held up her camera. "I've got my Kodak. I won it at the Fourth of July. I didn't see you there. Where were you? I could take your photograph." Never mind that it couldn't really take pictures.

"We were over at the auto races in Cedar Rapids with our families," said Mary Louise.

"Eight thrilling events," said Mary Alice. "Much more fun than that silly picnic."

"We've all got Kodaks," said Mary Helen. "Boring."

"And," added Mary Alice, "Mr. Moore says he's going to put our photograph in the first edition of the *Goodhue Progress,* due to the generous contributions our fathers made."

"We can't come anyhow," said Mary Louise. "My mother is going to give us bobs."

"Oh!" said Tugs. "But your hair is so beautiful already."

The Marys giggled at that and tromped on the grass to get around Tugs and Ned. Then they glided away. Tugs looked after them, holding her camera in front of her.

"Click," she said.

Bobbed

Back at home, Tugs left Ned in the living room with Granny and her mother and went to her room with the excuse that she had to change clothes. How could she be like the Marys with Ned hovering around?

She sat on her bed with her camera and scanned her room through the viewfinder, inspecting everything through the lens.

Click: a spider resting in her web in the sloped corner of the ceiling.

Click: tiny faded flowers on the curtain, rustling slightly in the barest midday breeze. The curtains were frayed at the bottom, and dirty.

There were several yellowed newspaper pictures cut from the *Cedar Rapids Tribune*.

She scanned the whole room but could not find one beautiful thing.

Until the Fourth of July, Tugs hadn't known she wanted a ribbon or a Kodak. She hadn't thought about possibility. Tugs had never aspired. Burton's accusation rang again in her head. Tugs *was* a Button, and all at once she understood what that meant. Who else but a Button would wear dirty ribbons pinned to their dirty overalls? Her face burned with belated embarrassment.

"What on earth are you still doing in here?" said her mother, peering around the door. "Ned wants to entice Granny into a game of marbles, but she's retreated out to the weed patch."

"Tell him I don't have time for him," said Tugs. "I'm busy."

Mother Button stepped all the way into Tugs's room and shut the door behind her.

"Busy is doing something useful. Now,

your cousin is here. I suggest you get out there and do something with him. You've got one foot in the doghouse already, leaving him with Ralph Stump for the three-legged race."

"I can't," said Tugs.

"What do you mean, can't?"

"I don't have anything to wear."

"Wear? Since when did you worry about what you are going to wear?"

"Girls wear dresses and skirts, Mother. I can't go around wearing those dirty overalls anymore."

Mother Button studied Tugs, then pulled open the middle dresser drawer and pulled out a dress.

"Here. You can press this. It probably still fits."

"Oh!" said Tugs. "I forgot about that dress. Thanks."

Tugs bounded out of bed and pulled on the dress in its wrinkled state and smoothed it with her hands. It was an old dress of her mother's that had been made over for Tugs for last year's school program. She'd stuffed it in the drawer afterward, never intending to wear something so uncomfortable again. It was a little small but she could still button it, and if she scrubbed the dirt off her knees, maybe no one would notice that it was a little too short. Why did she have to keep growing, for Pete's sake?

"There," she said, presenting herself to Mother Button and Ned in the living room. "All I need now is a bob. Can you cut my hair, Mama?"

Mother Button looked at Ned, who shrugged.

"It's the Marys," he said. "She wants to look like the Marys."

"Hmmm," mused Mother Button, running her fingers through Tugs's mass of curly hair. "Is that how the girls are wearing it now? I guess we could see what we could do." She rummaged through the junk drawer for a scissors and went to the linen closet for a sheet to put under the stool. "Just straight across all the way around, right?" she asked.

"Here," said Ned, holding up Mother Button's *Good Housekeeping* magazine. "Look at the pictures of the ladies in here."

Tugs thanked Ned grudgingly. She was grateful for the haircut help but annoyed that Ned was hanging around in the first place. Didn't he have friends his own age to bother? She paged quickly through the magazine.

"There," she said, pointing to a woman in an ad. "Like that. To the bottom edge of my face."

"Looks easy enough," said Mother Button. "Go wet your hair in the sink and we'll give it a try."

Tugs stuck her head under the kitchen sink and got it soaking wet. Then she wrapped a towel around her head and hopped up on the stool. Mother Button worked a comb through the snarls as Tugs winced. Then she pulled a lock of hair down with the comb, stopping the comb at chin length, then snipping along the teeth of the comb. She grabbed the next lock and repeated the process. Trouble was, when she let go of the wet hair, the spring in the curls wound right back up, leaving Tugs's new cut considerably shorter than anticipated. It was more of an ear-length bob than a chin-length bob. Ned's eyes grew wide.

"Well?" said Tugs, anxious to see.

"It's bobbed all right," said Ned.

"Oh, dear," said Mother Button. "I'm afraid this might not be exactly what you had in mind. But Ned is right. It *is* bobbed." She went to her room and brought back her hand mirror and held it up for Tugs to see.

"Perfect!" said Tugs. "I'll bet the Marys got theirs short, too. Wait until Aggie sees!" She shook her head back and forth. "I feel so light. Oh, my neck is all cool. You should try it, too, Mama. It's fashionable *and* comfortable."

"Well, one bob in the family might be

enough for starters," said Mother Button. "Get the broom, now, and sweep up all that hair."

"But I need to go to Mary Louise's."

"Tomorrow," said Mother Button firmly. "Your hair won't grow overnight, and if you change out of your dress for the rest of today, it will still be clean tomorrow."

Namesake

Tugs thought about what she would say when she got to Mary Louise's. She didn't have any real excuse for arriving uninvited, except to show off her new hair. She imagined them giggling over their matching haircuts. She could take a picture of all of them. Except that she left her Brownie at home. Maybe the Marys would let Tugs be an honorary Mary. And Aggie, too. The Five Marys. She would suggest it. Mary Louise, Mary Helen, Mary Alice, and . . . Tugs. Mary Tugs?

And with that thought, her avalanche of dissatisfaction welled. Mary Tugs sounded terrible. She said it out loud. Mary Tugs.

Ridiculous. Aggie, Louise, Helen, and Alice, now, those were girl names.

If she could change her name it would be . . . it would be . . . well, something lovely. Penelope? No. Catherine? No. Priscilla. Mary Priscilla. Perfect.

Tugs's actual name was a mistake to begin with. Her mother had been out at the Goodhue cemetery, which was a beautiful place, especially the part where the soldiers were buried. Their plots had little gold stars on gold sticks stuck in the ground next to the stones. The grass grew high there, and wildflowers bloomed whenever and wherever they wanted. There were wide shady trees and breezes on top of the hill.

It was one of Tugs's favorite places to roam, so it wasn't hard to imagine her own mother wandering there some hot summer day, trying to catch a breeze on her bare neck.

The way her mother told it, she was strolling the cemetery the week Tugs was born, when an early heat spell swept across the plains. She was so round and unwieldy she couldn't make it to the top of the hill, much as she craved that breeze. So she'd plopped her big self down to rest her back against a cool stone. After she'd sat there awhile, the cool of that stone had sunk into her back and she felt refreshed and hopeful that this baby would be her first living baby. Two had died before Tugs, but that was just the way of it. So Mother Button had turned around to read that headstone and give a little thank you to the soldier who had cooled her off and given her hope. The stone had grown mossy since the boy's death in 1864.

She read the name out loud. *Tugs Button,* she read. Well! A Button! What were the chances of that? Far as she knew, none of her husband's family had fought in the Civil War. Granddaddy Ike's drummer-boy days were a wee exaggerated, as the conflict ended before his drumming fingers had even gotten blistered. Far as she knew, there were no heroes among the Buttons.

She rose to her feet and lumbered back along the road as fast as she could, the baby kicking in her stomach to beat the band, and the heat not bothering her at all. She couldn't wait to tell Father Button.

He was incredulous. "Maybe he's from another branch of Buttons," he said. "Doesn't sound like our people."

"I know," said Mother Button. "But I saw it with my own eyes, and that is going to be the name of our baby." After all the babies they'd christened and buried, after all the tears he'd seen his wife shed, he was not going to say a word about what they'd name this one, though he hoped this baby would stick around awhile. But what if . . . ?

"What if it's a girl?" he asked.

"Pshaw," said Mother Button. "We haven't had a girl yet, not much chance of us starting now."

And Tugs was born that night and she was a girl. She was a wailer right away. They named her Tugs Esther, after the soldier and

Mother Button's favorite Bible woman. "It's grown on me already," she said of the name when people inquired about the odd moniker. "It'll grow on everyone else, too."

She told the story of the cool comfort of the brave soldier's tombstone every time she told anyone her baby's name, but no one else visiting the cemetery could ever find that stone. Granddaddy Ike had gone so far as to read back issues of the *Goodhue Gazette,* which, until its demise, he'd collected on his back porch. But he found no news of any other branch of Buttons, not even of Granddaddy Ike's own Civil War participation.

So on Tugs's first birthday, the little Button family had gone out to the cemetery, this time with a live baby. Mother Button wanted to show Father Button the stone and prove to him what a good upstanding name it was, even though he'd never said he didn't believe her.

"See?" she said. "See?" She pulled Tugs

close and held her tiny fingers up to trace the letters on her namesake's stone.

"Well, I never!" she exclaimed, and drew her own and Tugs's fingers back. She stood and looked around. "I must be remembering wrong," she said.

Father Button stooped down to look.

"*Thos. Britton,*" he read. "Thomas. You know, dear, at a glance, it kind of does look like Tugs. You see how the *h* here got rubbed away and the *s* is all swirly? And the *r* and *i* are faded out, too. It's a mistake anyone could make."

Mother Button let go of Tugs's hand and looked every which way.

"Oh, Robert," she said, struck with horror at what she'd done. The name she'd treasured this whole year, the name that had tripped off her tongue, sounding to her ears like a bird's song for twelve whole months — *Tugs Button, Tugs Esther Button* — was a mistake. She heard at once its gray tones, the flat guttural sound everyone else must have heard every time she said her baby's name.

"Oh, Robert," she said again. She looked at Tugs. "I'm sorry, baby," she said. Tugs babbled happily. Mother Button looked at Father Button. "Let's call her Esther. She's young. She won't even remember."

"Aw, honey," said Father Button. "Let it be. Tugs is a fine name."

But Mother Button's mind was made up. For the next month she caught herself every time she went to call Tugs and called her Esther, though it often came out Testher. She made up singsong rhymes and chanted the name to her baby constantly. But Tugs never responded. She'd repeat the sounds of the rhymes in her baby voice, but when they asked her what her name was, she said Tugs every time.

So the name stuck.

And from then until the moment Tugs approached Mary Louise's house, she had liked her name, even defending it to the numbskulls who taunted her about it. *I am named for a brave soldier of the Civil War,* she'd say. *We wouldn't even be the United States of America without the original Tugs Button.* She started improvising in about first grade and asking questions of Granddaddy Ike about the Civil War and adopting whatever facts she found exciting or interesting or particularly brave into her story about the first Tugs Button.

Perhaps she could tell Mary Louise that her middle name was Priscilla. Surely someone like Mary Louise would want other girls to have names as lovely as her own.

The Thompson Twins

Mary Louise lived on the other side of the Thompson twins. Tugs passed the library, tempted to go in and look up *Priscilla* in the dictionary, hoping desperately that it was a word, that it meant something, but the two sisters were out on their porch waving furiously.

"Leopold is stuck in the apple tree!" they hollered. "Help us get him down!"

Tugs hesitated. She really wanted to get to Mary Louise's house, but no one could say no to the insistent mews of that orange mound of feline.

Leopold outsized most raccoons. His belly hung so low he collected all manner of leaves and ground scraps, which he then left on the library carpet every time someone let his shaggy self through the door. You could always tell where Leopold had been when you went into the library, as there was a trail of leaves and grass marking his path, like Hansel and Gretel's crumbs. Usually he went to the children's area, because he got lots of attention there until somebody's mother shooed him out. Then he went scurrying in a straight line for the door, mewing as if maimed.

How a cat that fat had gotten himself up in the apple tree Tugs couldn't imagine. But sure enough, there he was, the tiny sisters carrying on beneath the tree.

"Whose girl are you?" demanded one.

"What happened to your head? You should put a hat over that mop!" said the other.

"She looks familiar. Is she a Lindholm, do you suppose? A Stump?"

Tugs smoothed her hair with one hand.

She could never tell the Thompson twins apart. Before Tugs could answer their questions, the second one admonished the first. "I don't see how it matters whose girl she is. She has long arms. She's tall. She looks like she could climb a tree."

Tugs had fallen out of her share of trees, but Leopold was on the lowest limb. Still, tiny as the two sisters were, they couldn't reach him.

"We've called and called," the one said indignantly. "I don't know why he doesn't come down."

"He hasn't eaten all day," said the other. "He's never climbed this tree before."

"He's never climbed any tree before."

"He never strays off this porch."

Tugs knew different but didn't say anything. The sisters didn't see too sharply through their thick glasses. Tugs had seen Leopold at the library, up trees, and sauntering as far away as the Ward's Ben Franklin. She didn't know where the sisters thought he was during those long absences. Maybe they had a fat sofa pillow that they thought was simply Leopold sleeping.

Tugs stood underneath the apple tree and looked up at Leopold. He hissed at her.

"What are you doing to him?" one sister gasped.

"Nothing, ma'am!" Tugs exclaimed. "I'm just looking at him."

"Well, do it quieter. Leopold is delicate. Loud noises upset him."

Tugs laughed but then saw that the sisters were serious. They were not aware that Leopold was the king of chaos. When he sauntered into the church on hot Sunday mornings, he'd sing right along with the rest of the congregation. And whine to beat the band when the singing stopped, which is when some usher or another would be forced to escort him from the building and close the door to the hope of a breeze.

She stood there a moment longer, then reached out her arms fast and grabbed

Leopold. He yowled but she held him tight, staggering under the weight of him. Tugs delivered Leopold to the front porch.

"No, no, inside," demanded one sister, escorting Tugs through the door held open by the other sister.

"Here," she said, patting the middle cushion on the sofa. "He likes this spot best."

As soon as Tugs loosed her grip, Leopold bolted for the bathroom, where he could be heard lapping water from the commode.

"Oh, dear," tittered the two sisters together.

"The poor thing must have been *so* thirsty. I hope you flushed, Elmira."

"Eldora!" gasped Elmira. "Not in front of the C-H-I-L-D."

"I'm sure she can spell, dear."

As they continued bickering, Tugs took in the room around her. She'd never thought to wonder what was inside the two sisters' house. She didn't know what she'd expected, but it wasn't this. On every surface were photographs in tiny ornate frames. On every wall between every window there were larger frames, all photographs. There were portraits and landscapes and pictures of Leopold. There were pictures of the sisters when they were young.

There were cameras lined up on shelves, models Tugs had never seen before. She wished she'd brought her Brownie.

She reached out her hand to touch one of the cameras.

"Don't touch!" screeched Eldora.

Tugs snapped her arm back to her side and took a step back.

"I'm sorry!" she said.

"Now you've gone and scared the child," said Elmira. "And she just rescued our Leopold." Elmira took down the camera and handed it to Tugs.

"Isn't it a beauty?" she said. "That one was my very first. Eldora got one, too—we always got everything at the same time—but she dropped hers and it broke. So we had to share this one."

"I dropped mine, too," said Tugs, turning the camera over in her hand. "But it doesn't look like this one. I won it at the Independence Day raffle."

"So you have yourself a Brownie," said Elmira. "We have fourteen Brownies between us, Eldora and me. We love the Brownies. When they came out in colors this year, we each bought a blue one. Here, we keep them in the kitchen. Come see."

Tugs forgot about the Marys then. She forgot about her clunky name, her bobbed hair, even G.O. and Harvey Moore. Eldora and Elmira were thrilled to have an interested audience. They guided Tugs through their camera collection and their photographs like docents at a museum. And for Tugs it *was* like going to a museum. Only better because she got to touch things.

"We used to be famous," said Eldora.

"In a Goodhue kind of way," said Elmira.

"Yes, when there was a newspaper in Goodhue, we took the photographs."

"Really?" said Tugs.

Eldora went to the pantry and pulled a tall album out from between the jars of beans and tomatoes. She opened it on the table.

"See for yourself." She pointed to a clipping of a somber-looking man who looked familiar to Tugs.

"This is Mr. Jackson," said Elmira. "We had our cameras with us, as usual, and we were sitting in a booth down at Al and Irene's across from Mr. Jackson, who bought us a nip now and again, didn't he used to do that, Sissy?"

"Sure, he did," said Eldora. "Mr. Everett came running through the door to report the death of President McKinley, and Mr. Jackson's face went like this here." She tapped her finger on Mr. Jackson's countenance. "And I just held up my Kodak and . . . click."

"The newspaper, they liked those sorts

151

of photographs. Raw emotion, they call it. And not many people had cameras in those days. We snapped a few more around town that day, then made them up and brought them down to the newspaper office, and there you have it."

"Paid us, too, they did," added Elmira.

"Now we don't have a paper," said Eldora. She shook her head. "Too bad, too."

"The library has copies of all of the old papers, though," said Elmira. "We visit them sometimes."

"And thanks to yours truly, we're going to have a new newspaper in town. How about that?"

"A new . . . ?" Tugs started.

"Why, yes, that dashing gentleman was here just yesterday, or day before."

"Dashing gentleman?" Tugs asked.

"What was his name, Sissy?" said Eldora. "Ford? Door?"

"Moore?" said Tugs. "Was his name Harvey Moore?"

"That's the one!" said Elmira.

"Such a nice man," said Eldora.

"What did he want?" asked Tugs.

"Want? Why, he didn't want anything. He was here to offer us an opportunity. We said we'd have to think about it, of course, but he said we could exchange our late daddy's (bless his soul) shares of Standard Oil for a founding share of his new venture. A newspaper! Imagine. He thinks two old ladies could be at the forefront of progress."

"Mr. Millhouse down at the bank is going to change our securities for cash. Mr. Moore is stopping back to collect before he goes back to Chicago to get the printing press and such."

"He took quite a shine to Leopold, too," said Elmira.

"Oh, but Leopold was being naughty. He diddled on that nice man's shoe. Leopold is particular about people, but not usually that particular."

"Now, what about your pictures?" said

Elmira, abruptly changing the subject. "Can we see yours?"

"I don't know how to get them out of the camera," said Tugs.

"Heavens to Mergatroid," said Eldora, laughing. "You mean that old Pepper gave you a Brownie but didn't tell you how to get the photographs developed? Wasn't there an instruction manual?"

Developed, thought Tugs. That's the word for it. *Developed.*

"That would be just like him, now, wouldn't it?" said Elmira. "Flinty Pepper. He could have at least given you a free round of developing. Nope. I thought it was unusually generous for Pepper to donate cameras for the raffle. He was just drumming up new customers, that's what. Once a fella or a lady owns a camera, what do they need but film and developing? And then more film. More developing. And talking to Pepper, you'd think there's no way to develop photographs but in his top-secret back room. The magic room, he calls it, like he's some sort of wizard holding the magic spell. There's nothing to it, really."

"Are you going to show her, Sissy?" Eldora broke in.

"I don't see why not," said Elmira. "She did save our Leopold."

"Show me what?" asked Tugs.

"Come to the back room, dear. Mind the step."

"And if you hear a *scritchety, scratchety,* that's just the mice Leopold has yet to catch. There's a hole back here somewhere, but they're mostly friendly."

"Do you have the flashlight, Sissy?" asked Elmira.

"Of course, Sissy. Now, here, you follow Elmira and me. Shut the door behind you."

They went through the kitchen and squeezed past the icebox to a small door.

"This used to be the extra pantry," said Elmira. "We made it over."

"Watch your head, now," Eldora said.

"We've got the window covered and there's a clothesline hanging across."

Elmira swept the flashlight beam around the small room, and in its path, Tugs saw a narrow table with tubs on top of it. Photographs were hanging from the clothesline strung wall to wall. Others were tacked onto the wall. Tugs was mesmerized.

Elmira shone the light on Tugs's face. "She likes it!" said Elmira, giggling. "Just like if we'd had a girl of our own."

"You know those aren't undies hanging from the line, don't you?" Eldora giggled.

Tugs nodded.

"It's the pictures," squealed Elmira, delighted with herself. "We have ourselves our very own darkroom."

"Oh, and doesn't it make Mr. Pepper mad!" tittered Eldora. "All that business, his best customers we were, whoosh out the door."

Tugs was desperate to see the photographs hanging on the line. She reached out her hand for the flashlight. Elmira handed it to her. She walked along the row of photos, studying each one. The first was the apple tree in the backyard. Since the sisters were so small, it was taken from underneath the lowest branch and was a view up into the limbs. The second was a similar picture — so similar, in fact, that Tugs couldn't tell the difference between them, save for a smudge down at the edge of one. The third was the same, only a little bit lighter. She went on down the row, puzzled at the repeated images.

"Aren't they lovely?" asked Eldora.

"She's speechless!" said Elmira. "Wouldn't old Pepper be jealous?"

Tugs did not point out that Mr. Pepper appeared to be plenty of years younger than either of the sisters, or that as far as she could tell his business was running just fine, or that these pictures were all the same, just a view of some backyard branches.

"Nice," was all she said. Clearly that was not high enough praise, because the sisters were disappointed in her reaction.

"*Nice,* she says!" sniffed Elmira.

"I think it's time for my midday repast," said Elmira.

"She means it's time for you to go," said Eldora to Tugs.

"I'm sorry if I . . ." Tugs started, but the sisters were already on their way out of the room, pulling Tugs with them.

They stood awkwardly in the living room. Tugs patted the sleeping Leopold's head and then boldness overtook her.

"Would you develop my photographs?" The sisters paused, door open to excuse her. "I took one of the dashing gentleman," she offered.

"Well, Sissy. She did rescue our Leopold."

"Yes, Sissy. I suppose you're right. And the gentleman is handsome."

"Come back tomorrow," said Elmira, and shooed Tugs out the door.

Tugs stood on the porch and remembered about Mary Louise and her plan to become a Mary, which made her remember her hair. She reached up and felt its shortness, already missing the pull of its former weight. She wished she could see the picture she'd taken of herself at the picnic.

Dapper Jack

Tugs stopped in at the library. She wanted to ask Miss Lucy for the old newspapers, but Mrs. Goiter, Miss Lucy's sometime substitute, was at the desk today. She couldn't possibly ask Mrs. Goiter for help. Mrs. Goiter eyed young hang-abouts with suspicion, shushing their every cough and snicker.

Tugs had been known to lose a book or two, but they were always — well, usually — found eventually, and while Miss Lucy was discrete about it, Mrs. Goiter had on more than one occasion called out in a loud voice, "Tugs Button! I'm going to confiscate your card!" or, "Tugs Button, you're on my list!"

Tugs slipped over to the dictionary to

think. *Priscilla* was not listed. She paged through, reading idly.

Atoll: a coral island or islands, consisting of a belt of coral reef, partly submerged, surrounding a central lagoon or depression; a lagoon island.

Lagoon: a shallow sound, channel, pond, or lake, especially one into which the sea flows; as, the lagoons of Venice.

Reef: a chain or range of rocks, coral, or sand, projecting above the surface at low tide or permanently covered by shallow water.

Tide: the twice daily rise and fall of the water level in the oceans and seas; to drift with or to be carried by the tides.

Tugs loved how one word led to another. She'd never seen an ocean, a lagoon, a reef, not even a mass of rock larger than the boulder that prevented Uncle Edgar from plowing the front acre, as he told the story. But one thing could lead to another, after all.

Then she paged back to *button,* as she often did.

> **Button:** a catch, of various forms and materials, used to fasten together the different parts of dress, by being attached to one part and passing through a slit, called a buttonhole, in the other; used also for ornament.

Then she flipped to *tug,* for Tugs.

> **Tug:** to pull or draw with great effort; to draw along with continued exertion; to haul along; to tow; as, to tug a loaded cart; to tug a ship into port.

> *"There sweat, there strain, tug the laborious oar."*
> — *Roscommon*

She repeated the small poem to herself. Tugs loved the strong images of her name.

She liked to think of herself towing things along. She would walk up to Mrs. Goiter and ask about newspapers.

Tugs took one more glance at her name in the book, then slipped her hand under the cover and folded it shut with a slap that was louder than she intended.

"Oh!" she exclaimed to no one in particular. "That was loud!"

"Tugs Button," bellowed Mrs. Goiter, stalking heavily through nonfiction and reaching Tugs in fewer than eight strides. She put her hands on her hips. "I'm trying to run a *library* here. This is a house of *quiet* and *decorum*. What are you doing and what do you want?"

Tugs wavered. She backed up to the pedestal table and rested her hand on the dictionary. "I . . ." she started.

"Well, out with it!" Mrs. Goiter barked, stepping close enough now that Tugs could smell her stale breath.

"N-n-newspaper?" Tugs stammered. "Old newspapers? I want to see pictures that the Thompson twins took."

"Humph." Mrs. Goiter shook her head and rolled her eyes to the ceiling. "Would you look at the dust on those lights? Do I have to do everything myself?" She shook her head again and walked away.

"Well?" she called in a sharp, very not-library voice, and turned with her hands on her hips. "This way."

Tugs hurried after her. They went down the curved stairway to a basement room that Tugs had not been in before. There were shelves and shelves of magazines and newspapers in stacks.

Mrs. Goiter motioned with a ruler. "Back issues. Locals on the right, more exotic fare to the left." She handed Tugs the ruler.

"To mark your place in the stack. Get anything out of order in here and it will be your last visit."

Tugs approached the rightmost shelf and

ran her hand across a stack of papers. Tentatively, she pulled the top one out partway and stood on her tiptoes to read the date. The *Cedar Rapids Tribune,* "A Newspaper Without a Muzzle." Friday, June 28, 1929. She skimmed the headlines. "No Excuse for Mine Disasters Says Uncle Sam," she read. She pulled the paper off the shelf. Near the bottom was a drawing of children watching fireworks, with the caption "Safe and Sane." Tugs wanted to explore the rest of the pages, but the *Cedar Rapids Tribune* wasn't what she was looking for. She slid it back on the stack and looked on a lower shelf. *Tribune, Tribune, Tribune.* Tugs moved left to another stack, then another, cautiously lifting papers and squaring them back so Mrs. Goiter wouldn't notice they'd been disturbed.

The *Gazettes* would be older than all of these papers. Or maybe they were counted in Mrs. Goiter's more exotic fare. She slid a paper off the top shelf. It was a Chicago paper. Nope. Then Tugs pulled it out again.

A Chicago paper, right there in the Good-hue library. Now, that was something. Aunt Fiona was the only Button brave enough to have explored a city larger than Cedar Rapids. What went on in Chicago that didn't go on in Cedar Rapids or Goodhue?

Tugs took the paper, laying the ruler in its place. She laid it flat on the table, admiring the large, smart type of the headlines.

"Scouts to Entertain Community" and "Two Escape Death as Train Hits." There was a cartoon of a man with a suitcase labeled "agriculture" buying a train ticket to Washington, D.C. She opened the newspaper. There were several photographs here. Her eyes skipped from one to another. She was about to turn the page when her eyes went back to a photograph in the corner. There was something familiar about it. The headline above it read "Dapper Jack Disappears with Dough." It was something about the smile. . . . Tugs read the article below it.

DAPPER JACK DISAPPEARS WITH DOUGH

Well-known Denver Bunco Gang member Jack Door, known by swooning ladies as Dapper Jack, should more likely be called Scamming Jack. Spotted at area establishments last month, as reported here in the *Herald*, it appears that Dapper Jack has wielded his charms on the unsuspecting citizens of several small communities outside Chicago, enticing trusting souls into all manner of business opportunities promised to improve their lives. Mr. Door made off with the life savings of several gentlemen and ladies as well as the accumulated weekly receipts of at least one business. Anyone seeing Mr. Door, whose known aliases include but are not limited to Johnny Shore, Henry Core, and Harvey Drew, should contact authorities at once.

Tugs looked again at the photograph. *Could it be?* He wasn't wearing a hat in the picture, but that too-wide smile was all too familiar. Harvey Drew, Jack Door. Harvey Moore. Tugs looked up from the paper. She was alone in the room. She could hear the heavy clump of Mrs. Goiter's shoes above her head. Tugs carefully tore the picture and article out of the paper, folded it, and put it in her pocket. Then she closed the paper, checking the edges to make sure it looked as if it hadn't been disturbed. Her hands shook as she carried it back to the shelf, removed the ruler, and laid the paper carefully on the stack where she'd found it.

Upstairs, she slid the ruler onto the check-out desk and walked as fast as she could toward the door, then ran three blocks before slowing down.

Developments

The next morning, Tugs wrapped up two
pieces of her mother's crumb cake in a
kitchen towel for the Thompson twins. She
grabbed her Brownie and slipped past sleeping Granny. How could the Marys think
cameras were boring? And who needed to
be hemmed in by a dress?

Tugs stopped at the curb to look back
at her house through the lens of her Kodak.
The shutters were akimbo. The paint was
peeling. She hadn't noticed before how
homely her home was. But as she walked
down the block, she saw that theirs wasn't
the only tired-looking house. Theirs wasn't
the only scrubby yard.

"Tugs! Wait up!"

Tugs turned. Ned was running after her. Ralph Stump was with him.

"My mom sent me to get you," said Ned. "Granddaddy's waiting on you."

Granddaddy Ike! It was Wednesday. Checkers day. Tugs hesitated. She really wanted to get her pictures developed. Maybe just this one week. . . .

"Do you think you could take him, Ned? Maybe he'll let you sit in on a game."

"Really? I always wanted to be the one to take him, but you've always been the one and —"

"It's a big responsibility," Tugs said, interrupting him. "You'd have to watch out for him. And make sure he doesn't put in your mother's silver or —"

"I know," said Ned. "I can do it. Ralph and I can, can't we, Ralph?"

"I don't have a granddaddy as old as yours, so I don't know," said Ralph.

"Well, we can," said Ned. "Thanks, Tugs. I won't let you down. Come on, Ralph."

Tugs watched them run off. For a moment, she wished Ned was coming with her. But it was good he had Ralph. She had Aggie, after all. At least she hoped she had Aggie. She'd show Aggie her photographs when she got home from camp.

Eldora and Elmira were sitting on their porch of their smart, well-kept house when Tugs passed the library. Leopold was perched in a potted plant in front of the library, and as she passed, he jumped out and followed her up the walk to the house.

"Sissy!" exclaimed Elmira. "Looky here, looky here! Our Leopold has been rescued again! Thank you, young man."

"Oh, Sissy!" cried Eldora. "Our Leopold!"

"I didn't . . ." Tugs started, but the sisters were down the steps and scooping up Leopold between them.

"He's been gone since breakfast and we feared the worst, didn't we, Sissy?"

"Oh, my, yes, Sissy. Our Leopold never runs off, and when we sat down in our porch chairs like we do every morning after toast and bacon, with our cup of coffee like every morning, our Leopold did not come sit by our feet like he does every morning." Eldora sighed into Leopold's shaggy back as he struggled to get free.

"I said to Sissy, I said, 'This could be the day we say good-bye to our faithful friend,'" said Elmira. "But you've saved him." She looked more closely at Tugs. "Why, you aren't a young man at all. You are the girl who got him out of the tree, aren't you?"

Eldora pushed her glasses up on her nose and peered closer at Tugs.

"That's her, Sissy. The very one. It's the pants that threw us off."

"I brought cake!" Tugs said. "And my camera. Remember you said you'd develop my film?"

"Cake!" said Elmira.

"She did bring back Leopold," said Eldora.

"True enough," said Elmira.

"Give me the Kodak, then," said Eldora.

"And the cake," said Elmira.

Tugs followed the sisters inside and sat on the sofa. They took the chairs across from her and leaned forward, staring at her like she was a show about to start.

"Well, I never," said Elmira, taking the Brownie from Eldora and inspecting it. "She's got herself a green F model. Old Pepper only had the blue, so he said. But we really wanted the green."

"Looks like she's dropped it," said one.

"It's a little banged up," agreed the other.

Elmira held it up to the light and looked through the lens.

"Should still work, though. These are sturdy little boxes. I bet it's just a broken mirror. We must have a spare around here we could fix in its place."

"Oh, Sissy, won't this be fun! I wonder what she photographed!"

"I . . ." Tugs started, but Eldora interrupted.

"No, don't tell! It's more fun to be surprised."

"Yes!" agreed Elmira. "I do love a surprise. That is the best part. When we take photographs, we develop each other's film. Eldora mine and I hers. Then we're always surprised."

"Except that she always tells me when she's taken a photograph," said Eldora. "Can't keep a secret, that one."

"Pshaw," argued Elmira.

"Can I help?" asked Tugs.

"No," said Elmira. "Not enough room. You wait here with Leopold. Come on, now, Sissy, let's see what she's got here."

Tugs wandered the room. She took down cameras and held them in her hands, looking through their viewfinders, until she heard the creak of the darkroom door. She sat down quickly on the sofa.

"Here's your Brownie. We did fix the mirror," Eldora said. "Good as new. Though that dent is making some trouble for advancing the film. You'll have to fiddle with it a bit. Here. We have lots of extra film. Take a few rolls, so you can keep snapping."

"But the pictures?" insisted Tugs.

"Ah, yes, the pictures," said Eldora.

"Sissy loves the suspense, she does," said Elmira. "Let's put the poor child out of her misery. They're still drying. Come on back."

"The first one is really very nice," Eldora said, chattering on. "So much detail. So close up. Not at all blurry . . ."

But Tugs did not hear her. She stopped in front of the first photograph and saw her own face staring back. There were her big teeth, protruding, her thin lips barely stretched into a quizzical smile. There was hair popping out in every direction, a fat strand blown across her face. But most of all what Tugs saw were her own eyes staring back at her. Her eyes looked clear and bright. Friendly. They made her face the face of someone she'd want to be friends with.

"Hi," she said to the picture, and then they all laughed.

"She's kind of cute, that one," said Eldora, taking the photo from Tugs's hand.

But what about Harvey? She was sure her picture could prove he was really Dapper Jack Door.

She hurried down the line. Aggie was blurred as she spun away. The Rowdies were fuzzy in movement, too.

"Now, there's the gent," said Eldora, squeezing past Tugs to the last photo.

Tugs studied the photograph. Harvey Moore was holding his hat, and his face was clear for viewing.

"Let me see that again," said Elmira. "Isn't that Mr. Dashing?"

"Indeed it is. What was his name again?"

"He says it's Harvey Moore," said Tugs. "But I think he's really a crook. Dapper Jack."

"Really?" gasped Eldora.

"How exciting!" said Elmira.

"But how do you know?" asked Eldora.

"I found this article in the newspaper," said Tugs. She pulled the folded paper out of her pocket.

"Let's go back out where it's bright," said Eldora.

They laid the paper on the kitchen table near the window and studied it together.

"He does resemble our gentleman," said Elmira.

"What about Daddy's money?" said Eldora.

"I think he is taking people's money and he's going to leave town."

"What about the *Goodhue Progress*?"

"I don't think there is going to be a news-paper," said Tugs.

"If there's not going to be a newspaper, I don't want to give him our money!"

"No. You can't give him your money," said Tugs.

"I'm going to ring the police," said Eldora.

"Wait," said Tugs. "I want to be sure."

"What are we going to do when he comes to the house?" said Elmira.

"What are we going to do?" repeated Eldora.

"Don't answer the door for Mr. Moore," said Tugs. "I'll figure out something."

A Message

Mrs. Dostal was arguing with Granny over the fence when Tugs got home. Tugs took advantage of their distraction and knocked at the Dostals' door. Mr. Dostal answered wearing just his undershirt and pants and looking like he'd just woken up.

"Yep?" he said.

"Is Mr. Moore at home?"

"Nope," said Mr. Dostal.

Tugs sighed.

"OK," she said, and Mr. Dostal started to close the door.

"Do you know when he's going to be back?" she asked hopefully.

"Nope." Mr. Dostal started to close the door once more.

"Wait!" said Tugs. Mr. Dostal opened the door again and raised his eyebrows.

"Did he teach you to sail yet? Mrs. Dostal said he was going to teach you to sail."

"We don't have a lake," said Mr. Dostal. This time he left the door open but started to walk away.

"Did he fix your Ford?"

Mr. Dostal stopped, turned around, and came back to the door. He was looking a little more awake.

"No, he hasn't, now that you mention it. No, he has not. In fact, he hasn't fixed the sink, either, like he said, or picked up the tab for groceries, or repaid the small loan I gave him to send back home to his ailing mother. Well, I'll be jiggered."

"I was just wondering," said Tugs, and she walked down the steps and across the lawn to her own house, waving to Mrs. Dostal and Granny as she went in the door.

Her mother was waiting for her.

"Look," said Mother Button. "You got mail." She held out a crisp white envelope embossed along the edge with a line drawing of a tree and lake entwined with an address in small type.

Mail. Tugs had only gotten mail once before in her life when Aunt Fiona had sent her a postcard. Georgia was spelled out in fat letters across the front, and inside each one was a picture featuring some aspect of Georgia life, which, surprisingly, didn't look so different from life in Iowa. On the back was a note Tugs still knew by heart.

Dearest Niece,
Peach pie, pecan pie, cotton plants, ocean.
People of every sort. Home soon.
Love, AF

181

But this was an envelope, licked and sealed and stamped.

Tugs looked it over front and back. There was her own name, hand-printed smartly on the front. She handed it back to her mother, who slid a knife under the flap, making a neat slice at the top.

Tugs opened the edges of the envelope and peered inside. She pulled out a folded sheet of paper that matched the envelope. She sank into a kitchen chair and laid it flat on the table. Her eyes skimmed directly to the bottom of the letter.

"*Your friend, Aggie,* it says! Aggie Millhouse! Aggie wrote me a letter!"

"Would you fancy that?" said her mother. "Read the whole thing."

"*Dear Tugs,*" she read. "Dear!"

"Go on," said Mother Button. "That's how most letters begin."

Tugs smoothed the letter with her hand and read it again, silently.

Dear Tugs,

It is Monday. I'm at camp. They make us write letters here every day. I am writing to you first of my friends. It's hot here, but we get to swim in the lake. They make us do crafts, but there is also archery. I'm going to ask for a bow and arrow for my next birthday. I hit the hay bale five out of ten times, a record for beginners, they said. I wish you were here. I bet you'd be good at archery, too. I brought my ribbon from the three-legged. It's hanging on my bunk. See you in the funny pages.

Your friend,
Aggie Millhouse

"Well," said Mother Button. "You'd better write back. Granny has stationery around here somewhere." She walked to the door and called Granny.

Granny hobbled into the house and hung her cane over a kitchen chair. "She's going to write a letter to a Millhouse?" She wobbled around the room looking for her stationery box. "Who does she think she . . . ?"

Mother Button interrupted her. "Aggie Millhouse has written to Tugs from camp. We need some nice paper, now, Granny. The best you've got."

"It's *all* the best," Granny sniffed. "Here." She held out a long, thin box. "I suppose you'll want to use one of my nice ink pens, too."

"Oh, no," said Tugs, taking the box from Granny. "I'll use pencil. And an eraser."

She looked through the papers. There was white, cream, light blue, and green. She liked the green best, but Aggie, she thought, would prefer blue.

She pulled out one blue sheet and a matching envelope.

"What are you going to say?" asked Granny, standing over Tugs as she picked up her pencil. Mother Button stood by, too, watching.

"I don't know," said Tugs. "But I think I need to write it in private."

"Well!" said Granny.

"Let her be," said Mother Button. "Here, Tugs. Take a magazine to your room to write on."

Tugs took the *Good Housekeeping* and her paper and pencil to her room and shut the door.

She propped herself on her bed and poised her pencil over the page again. Aggie was just the person she needed to talk to. But how to start? Tugs set the stationary down and got up to move her ribbon from her dresser pull to her bedpost like Aggie's. There.

Dear Aggie,

My ribbon is hanging on my bed, too.

I liked it when you read my essay at the Fourth of July. Miss Lucy put my essay ribbon up at the library. But I took it down. Swimming and archery sound fun.

Do you remember on the Fourth of July when I said I had something important to tell you? It just got more important. I think Mr. Moore is not Mr. Moore at all but Dapper Jack Door, a crook from Chicago. I saw his picture in a newspaper. I think he is going to take your father's money and everyone else's and leave town without starting a newspaper. I don't know what to do.

When do you come home from camp? I hope it is soon.

Your friend,
Tugs Button

Tugs read over her letter three times. Then she folded it and put it in the envelope. She licked it shut and wrote *Aggie Millhouse* on the front. She copied the camp address from Aggie's envelope and went back to the kitchen.

"Well," said Granny. "Took you long enough. What did you say? Did you spell everything right? I'd better check it over."

"I already licked it," said Tugs. "Do we have any stamps?"

"Here," said Mother Button, rooting through the whatnot drawer. "Yes. Here we go. If you run down to the post office now, it may still go out with today's mail."

Alley Rat

Tugs ran out, letting the screen door slam behind her. Her legs carried her past Granddaddy's cottage and Ned's house, past a pair of snarling dogs and a wailing baby in a carriage. If she took the shortcut through Carl's Alley, she would avoid all of Main Street and come out right at the post office. Tugs usually avoided Carl's Alley because it was narrow and dark and the back doors of businesses opened onto it. There were piles of boxes and trash and always the threat of rats, whether real or imagined. But if she got to the post office in time, Aggie would get her letter tomorrow.

Tugs turned into the alley.

She heard a noise and stopped, straining her ears and waiting for her eyes to adjust to the dimness. She could turn around. But the letter. She was so close. It must have been her imagination. Then she heard it again. It was low voices, not rats. Just behind a pile of boxes, a clump of people huddled. Tugs stopped again, but she'd been spotted.

"Well, if it isn't the fancy writer!" said a familiar voice. "Where are you off to in such a hurry? Got a letter for the president?" It was Harvey Moore, with the Rowdies. G.O. Lindholm was there, too.

Tugs took a deep breath. She thought about Aggie Millhouse standing up to G.O. in her own alley. But this was G.O. and the Rowdies and Mr. Harvey Moore, and it was Carl's Alley. Her legs wanted to turn and run, but she resisted.

"Going to the post office. Mailing a letter for my mother. She writes letters all the time. Going to mail it to her. FOR her.

Urgent. Very urgent." She walked quickly, but Harvey Moore stepped in her path.

"Come join us," said Harvey. "We were just having a little fun."

Tugs looked nervously from Harvey to Luther to Bess and Finn and Frankie. Bess looked away. Finn and Frankie made a face at her.

"I can't stay. I have to get to the . . . I thought you were rats!" Tugs said. "I mean I didn't think you were rats when I saw you, but I thought . . . I mean, when I heard noises, and it's always dark here and . . ."

"Rats!" howled Harvey. "Did you hear that, gang? Rats. That's rich. I was just showing the fellows here a slick card trick. Let them try it out on you. Come on, who wants to be first?"

"Let her go," said G.O. quietly. Harvey turned sharply to G.O.

"What did you say?"

"Let her go," said G.O. again, a little louder. "She's going to be late for something."

Harvey looked hard at G.O., then back at Tugs. He laughed.

"What was I thinking? You're too young anyhow. You boys should practice on some regular folks. Let's go down to the pool hall. I've got a few fancy things I can show you there, too. Run along now, girly. Mail the letter for your mommy."

Tugs ran for the end of the alley and straight into the street. A Pontiac honked and screeched out of the way. Tugs looked down at the letter. She'd been holding it so tight, it was crumpled and dirty with the sweat from her hand. Nothing to be done about it now. She pulled open the heavy door and walked into the coolness of the post office.

"I'd like to mail a letter," she said to the clerk, holding out the blue envelope.

"You're just in time," said the clerk. "Hank! Wait up. Got one more here." He turned back to Tugs. "Relax," he said. "You made it. It's your lucky day."

Put Right

Tugs reached to push open the door, then stopped. Harvey Moore and the Rowdies were just passing. She stepped backward into the lobby. She read all the notices and Wanted posters on the wall. Then she read them again. She stood at the window and looked down the street. Life outside was going on like normal, people going about their business, while her world was one knotted mess.

"Anything wrong, young lady?" the clerk said.

Tugs hesitated. "No."

"Well, then, you'd better get along. Your mother is probably expecting you."

"Yes," said Tugs. "I just . . . Yes." She pushed open the heavy door and felt the hot air hit her face. She walked slowly down the steps.

"Tugs," came a voice from behind her. She jumped. It was G.O.

"Hold up!" he said. "I'm not after you."

G.O. slouched toward Tugs, his hands in his pockets.

"Thanks for sticking up for me back there," said Tugs. "But . . ."

"You don't have to worry about them. They're on their way to the pool hall with Mr. Moore. He's got some tricks to teach them. I'll walk with you if you want."

"Why aren't you with them?"

G.O. was quiet.

"Oh," said Tugs. "You shouldn't have said anything."

"Yep," he said. "Mr. Moore doesn't like people messing in his business."

"Why did you?"

"You saved me at the three-legged when

you hollered at Lester. My dad says pay back a bad deed once, a good deed twice. I guess I still owe you one."

"There is one thing," Tugs said, thinking about the Lindholms and their scavenging ways. "Do you think my camera box could be at your house? I left it at the park on the Fourth of July."

G.O. looked at the ground. His ears reddened.

"Probably it is," he said. "I'll see."

"OK," said Tugs. "But about Luther and them, I thought you wanted to be a Rowdy. You can't stir the pot like that if you want them to let you hang on."

"Yep, I know. But funning around is one thing. I just want to hang out with Luther and them. Have a smoke. Pal around. So I followed them to the alley today. But Mr. Moore was talking about doing some kind of work, anyhow, and that's not for me. Going to people's houses. My ma says to stay out of other people's houses or else.

Though earning some coin is tempting. Finn and Frankie said maybe they'd come by for me tomorrow, and maybe they'll let me help. I don't know."

"What kind of work was he talking about? Did he want them to do a crime?"

"Nah. Doesn't sound illegal. People said they'd give Mr. Moore money for the paper. Now he's got to collect it. But he's got to hustle back to Chicago in a couple of days, he says. And it's too much to do all on his own."

Tugs studied the pavement as they walked. *Collecting money at people's houses.* The Rowdies didn't know that the money wasn't really for the newspaper, and she was pretty sure Mr Moore would find a way out of paying them, too. She nearly felt sorry for the Rowdies. They didn't know a please from a thank-you. Most people probably wouldn't even open their doors.

"G.O.," said Tugs, "I don't think that money is for the newspaper at all."

"Then what's it for?"

"I think he is going to steal it."

G.O. whistled. "Try telling that to anyone in this town. No one will believe you. Everyone thinks Mr. Moore is the king's pajamas."

"My granddaddy Ike says that," said Tugs.

"Says what?"

"The king's pajamas."

"So does my dad," said G.O.

"But we have to tell someone," said Tugs. "If Mr. Moore is hustling back to Chicago, everyone will lose their money."

"Who are you going to tell?" asked G.O.

Tugs thought about the people she knew who could solve a problem. Aggie was the main one, and she'd written to Aggie. Thinking about Aggie made her think about her Fourth of July ribbons, which made her think about Miss Lucy and the display case. Miss Lucy was just the person. And she could watch out for the Thompson twins.

"We could tell Miss Lucy, at the library," said Tugs.

"I don't have a card," said G.O.

"That doesn't matter," said Tugs. "Come on!" Tugs turned to start for the library, then stopped abruptly. "But if it is too late to mail a letter, it's too late to go to the library today."

"It's probably all right," said G.O. "Who is going to hand over money to the Rowdies anyhow?"

"I was thinking that, too," said Tugs. "I guess it's OK. I'll tell my parents about Mr. Moore tonight. Just stay home tomorrow. Don't go out with the Rowdies."

"I don't know," said G.O. He turned to walk toward his house. "See you."

"And stay away from Mr. Moore," Tugs called after him.

Sequestered

"You think I like this any better than you do?" said Granny, poking a needle up through a circle of stretched fabric and handing it to Tugs. "I don't know how you managed to get yourself stranded here all day, but wipe that sour look off your face. This hurts me just as much as it does you."

It was Thursday morning. Tugs and Granny were sitting on the davenport, dutifully trying to master a needlepoint pattern Mother Button had pulled from a box of unfinished projects under her bed. Mother Button had gone to get the pie Aunt Mina was baking for the occasion of this predicament.

After Tugs's tale at dinner last night, she'd been admonished not to leave the house until her father took care of matters. Her mother had spent the rest of the evening lamenting—Tugs had too much freedom—and berating herself for not keeping a closer watch.

Tugs's story about Mr. Moore had come out in a jumble.

"Why would the librarian have stock in Standard Oil?" Granny had asked.

"Dapper *who*?" Mother Button kept asking.

And by the time Tugs sorted out the Thompson twins next to the library and G.O. and the Rowdies in Carl's Alley, everyone was thoroughly baffled.

"But he dresses too smartly to be a criminal," mused Mother Button.

"Says in Tugs's article that this Dapper Jack is a smart dresser," conceded Father Button. "And Mr. Dostal did say there is a lot of cash in a suitcase under Mr. Moore's bed. He's puzzled why Mr. Moore hasn't gone for his printing press with all that cash." Father Button didn't put much sway in town bigwigs, and he wouldn't want to consult a police officer, but given Tugs's insistence on the matter, he said he'd at least run it by Mayor Corbett, since he had repaired a windmill at the mayor's home after a storm summer before last and the mayor had said, if there was ever anything Robert Button needed . . .

"Ouch!" said Tugs. "I poked myself again." She sucked on the offended finger and tossed the needlework on the floor.

"If you've been injured, I think even your mother will agree that this is too dangerous a sport," said Granny. "What do girls like you like to do, anyhow?"

"I like to take pictures," Tugs said. "I'll get my Brownie."

Tugs let Granny hold her camera and described how all the parts work.

"If that don't beat all!" Granny exclaimed when Tugs showed her how to look through the viewfinder. "It's like real life, only tiny.

"Help me to my feet," Granny said. She stood and looked around the room through the camera, pausing when she came to Tugs.

"How do I take a photograph?" she said. Tugs put Granny's finger on the shutter lever.

"Now, stand back there," said Granny. "I'm going to capture your image."

Tugs stood stiffly and smiled for a long moment until she heard the click.

"Now me," Granny said. "But make me look good. Like Mary Pickford before she cut her hair."

Granny stood up tall, one hand resting on the back of a kitchen chair. She fixed her collar and smoothed her skirt.

"How's my hair?"

"Good," said Tugs. She looked down through the viewfinder and stepped closer, framing just Granny's face and shoulders. *Click*.

Mother Button bustled through the door and set a raspberry pie on the table.

"There," she said. "That's done. Now, how did this needlework get on the floor? Here, let me help you get back on track."

"No, Corrine," said Granny. "It was hurting my eyes, so Tugs said she would read to me. I'm just going to lie right down on this davenport and close my eyes." She winked at Tugs as she hobbled to the sofa. "Nothing too sweet," she said. "What do you have out from the library?"

"*The Bobbsey Twins in a Great City*," said Tugs. "I'll go get it."

"Well, I'm glad to see you two getting along so well," said Mother Button. "I was going to bring Ned back here to entertain you, but after I told Aunt Mina about Mr. Moore and the Rowdies, she thought it best to go find G.O. and bring him and Ned out to Uncle Elmer's farm for a couple of days. Some hard work will keep that Lindholm boy out of trouble. His mother was in Mina's and my class. Such a story. Such a story."

Tugs was relieved that G.O. was away from the Rowdies, but what would happen now? She peered through her curtains at the Dostals' house. Was Mr. Moore there right this minute? It made her cold inside just to think it. As she looked for her book, Tugs imagined her father's meeting with Mayor Corbett. Maybe the mayor would give her a ribbon for revealing Mr. Moore for a crook. Maybe there would be cake.

"Old lady ready for a story out here!" Granny hollered. Tugs grabbed her book and pulled up a chair next to Granny.

"I'm on chapter five," she said, opening to her marked page. "'Glorious News.'"

City Hall

The next morning, Tugs was consumed with scrubbing and hair washing. Mother Button worked on Tugs's hair with a wide comb and tried smoothing it with a bit of lard. Granny was enlisted to iron Tugs's dress, and Mother Button darned a pair of her socks.

Tugs stood in front of Mother Button's mirror.

"I don't look like me," she said.

"We'll have to put an apron on you while you eat lunch, or you'll look like you again in a wink."

"I'm not hungry anyhow," said Tugs. She picked her way through the meal, nodding without listening to Granny's noontime chatter. She couldn't even face pie. She jumped up when Father Button came home at last.

"No time like the present," he said. "Mayor said to drop by his office at one o'clock. Ready, Tugs?"

Tugs dropped her dishes in the sink and tossed her apron over a chair.

"Give 'em the what for," said Granny.

"Just tell the truth," said her mother.

Tugs grabbed her father's hand. She glanced over at the Dostals' house, but there was no sign of Harvey Moore, or Mr. or Mrs. Dostal, either.

"No one's home next door," she said, feeling lighter.

Father Button nodded. "Nope," he said.

"Do you think the mayor will give me a ribbon?" said Tugs. She skipped ahead of her father, then back. She didn't have patience for his slow and steady pace. Yesterday had been eternal, and Tugs was excited that the whole ordeal would be over with soon. She would write Aggie as soon as she got home and tell her not to worry.

"Don't get your hopes up," said her father. "I done my best, but all the mayor said was he'd look into it. Mayor Corbett likes the idea of that newspaper, and he's going to be reluctant to let it go."

"Did you show him the clipping? Did you tell him about the car? How Mr. Moore didn't know about it being out of gas until I told him? And about Carl's Alley and the Rowdies? And the Thompson twins and Standard Oil?"

"I told him what I could remember, Tugs. Now, just walk like a lady and we'll see what we see."

City Hall stood next to the post office. Tugs had never been inside. It wasn't a big building, but it had a heavy presence to it. They were a bit early, and the mayor's secretary was not at her desk. They could hear voices from inside the office.

"Should we knock?" whispered Tugs. They stood a moment, considering, then Tugs's father walked up to the door and gave a tentative knock. There was no answer, so he knocked again a bit louder.

Mayor Corbett himself swung the door open.

"Hello, Mayor!" Tugs beamed, eager to receive his praise. But the mayor's face was stern.

"Robert, Tugs," he said. He opened the door and gestured for them to follow him. Tugs stepped in eagerly, then stopped short. There, standing next to the mayor's desk, was Harvey Moore. For once, he was not smiling. He took off his hat and fiddled with the brim.

"Have a seat," Mayor Corbett said, gesturing to the two chairs facing his desk. Tugs edged into one and inched it closer to her father's. The mayor stood behind his desk, next to Harvey Moore.

"Robert, you did right telling me about

Tugs's accusations, and I'm glad you brought her down here today. It's a good thing you talked to me, not the rest of town. Rumors get started. Damage can be done."

"I don't understand," Father Button said, rising from his chair. "This man is not . . ."

Mayor Corbett motioned for him to sit, and looked at Tugs.

"Tugs, your father told me your story about Mr. Moore. You made some serious charges, young lady. Now, my job as mayor is to protect and serve all members of this community, and that includes residents, such as yourself, and guests, such as Mr. Moore here. I called Mr. Moore in and told him what you said. Showed him this clipping, which is thin evidence, indeed, to say nothing of the vandalism you perpetrated to get it." He slapped it down on his desk.

"I reviewed the facts. And while it embarrassed him to have to do it, Mr.

Moore provided me with a list of personal references to account for his character."

"But—" Tugs interrupted. The mayor held up his hand to silence her.

"But nothing, Tugs. I chatted with Mr. Moore, and I assured him I don't need to call his references. A man who can look another man in the eye and shake his hand firmly, that's a man that's telling the truth.

"Now, I don't know where your wild imagination came up with these preposterous claims, but I am very disappointed. Very disappointed, indeed, that a citizen like you, a patriotic essay winner, would try to stand in the way of progress.

"Do you know what *slander* means? Slander is a false report, one that can damage a person's reputation. In this case, it could even derail the publication of a town newspaper. Imagine if people heard your claims, pulled back their money.

"There needs to be consequences for

such behavior, Tugs. And I have asked Mr. Moore here to help me arrive at a suitable recompense."

Tugs looked questioningly over at her father. He reached out and took her hand. She slumped in her chair.

"Thank you, Mayor," Mr. Moore said, setting his hat on the mayor's desk. "Now, I don't want to be too harsh on the child, Mr. Button, but I'm sure you'll agree, my reputation *has* been damaged. There is the question of how many people she's entertained with this wild tale, for instance."

"Tugs?" her father asked. "Besides your mother and me, and Granny?"

Tugs ran through the list in her head. How could she face Aggie again? And what if the Thompson twins told Miss Lucy?

"Tugs!" Mayor Corbett was saying. "Are you listening?"

"I . . ." Tugs started, but a sharp rap at the door interrupted her.

"What now?" said Mayor Corbett. "Where *is* Miss Wert? She takes the longest lunches." There was another rap, then the door swung open.

Mr. Millhouse strode into the room, with Aggie just behind him.

"Tugs!" Aggie cried, and ran to Tugs.

"Aggie! I got your letter!"

"I know. I got yours, too."

"Mayor," said Harvey Moore briskly, "I see you have company. We can finish our business later." He slipped past Mayor Corbett.

"Mr. Millhouse," he said with a nod.

"Not so fast, Mr. Door," said Mr. Millhouse.

"Door?" repeated Mayor Corbett. "It's Moore. Harvey Moore. We're almost through here, then. . . ."

"I'm afraid you've been deceived, Mayor. This man is not Harvey Moore. If you'll all have a seat, including you, Mr. Door, I'll explain."

But Harvey Moore was already out the door.

"Don't worry, Mayor," said Mr. Millhouse. "Officer Miller and his men are waiting for him outside."

"I'm afraid I—I—I . . ." Mayor Corbett stuttered.

"He's a fraud, Mayor. A swindler. We got an emergency call from Aggie's summer camp yesterday. They said Aggie was sick and we should drive out and get her."

"Are you sick?" gasped Tugs, grabbing Aggie's arm.

"She's not sick," continued Mr. Millhouse. "Aggie, why don't you tell the story?"

"I got a letter from Tugs yesterday. She told me about seeing Mr. Moore in the Chicago paper, only he was the crook Mr. Door. She said how he is out to ruin my father and everyone else in Goodhue, too. I tried telling my camp counselors, but they thought I was spinning a yarn. I knew I had to tell my father right away, so I played sick so they'd call him."

"I admit I was skeptical at first," said Mr. Millhouse. "But I did put a call in to the Chicago police this morning, and what Tugs says is true. Harvey Moore is just one of many aliases used by Mr. Door as he travels to small towns like our own, swindles its citizens, and moves on. He's a slippery fellow, and there are a lot of people looking for him. I was deceived — we were all deceived — by a slick smile, a quick wit, and a story we wanted to believe."

Tugs looked from Mr. Millhouse to her father to the mayor.

"I'm flabbergasted," said Mayor Corbett, sinking into his chair. "Simply flabbergasted." Absently, he picked up the Panama Mr. Moore had left on his desk. "Well, look at that," he said wearily. He turned the underside of the hat toward them. An envelope was stitched into the crown.

Mayor Corbett pulled out a stack of bills, shaking his head in wonder.

Mr. Millhouse held out his hand to shake Father Button's.

"Mr. Button, I presume? You have a fine, fine daughter here. Tugs, you are welcome in our home anytime."

Tugs beamed. She had been right. And here was Aggie, better than in her picture.

Picture.

"Eldora and Elmira!" Tugs gasped. "Leopold!" She grabbed her father's hand. "We have to go!"

"Who?" said her father and Aggie at the same time.

"The ladies next to the library?" asked Mr. Millhouse.

"But who is Leopold?" said Mayor Corbett.

"The Rowdies! Oh, no. They don't know . . . They are going to . . ." continued Tugs.

"Slow it down, Tugs," said Mayor Corbett. "What *is* the matter?"

Tugs explained as quickly as she could about Mr. Moore, the Rowdies, and the twins.

Mr. Millhouse nodded grimly. "Yes, the Thompson twins. I was informed that they had withdrawn a large amount of cash. Well."

"I'll ring Officer Miller," said Mayor Corbett.

"He and his men are with Mr. Door," said Mr. Millhouse.

Father Button spoke up then. "Do you have your car, Mr. Millhouse? We should just go over there."

Tugs grabbed the clipping off Mayor Corbett's desk as they all hurried out to the street.

Lucky Button

"What on earth?" Mr. Millhouse said.

They slowed to a stop near the library.

"Well, I never," said Mr. Button, sitting between Mr. Millhouse and the Mayor.

"What? What?" said Aggie and Tugs from the backseat.

They piled out of the car.

Eldora and Elmira sat primly in their chairs on the porch, surrounded by Rowdies sitting on the steps and the porch rail, leaning against the house, all munching on cookies. Miss Lucy was there, too.

"It's our girl!" said Elmira, seeing Tugs. "I can tell by that wide hair."

"She brought a posse with her this time. Come join the party!" said Eldora.

"Meet our new friends," said Elmira. "These fellows rescued our Leopold! He'd gotten off to heaven knows where this morning and we were bereft."

"BeREFT!" Eldora echoed.

"We were inside making jam . . ."

"Truth be told, we were eating jam with a spoon . . ."

"Yes, well. We didn't hear a knock at the door, but we turned around and there were these two boys just alike. Look at them!" Elmira patted Finn's and Frankie's cheeks.

"They are so alike!" said Elmira. "Just like us. And so I said, 'Don't know how you got in here, but how about some jam?'"

"And the one said—I'll never forget, it was the sweetest thing—he said, 'We prefer cookies.'" The sisters laughed so hard, they had to pull out their hankies and dab at their eyes.

"We prefer cookies," repeated Elmira.

"Doesn't that just beat all? Of course they prefer cookies. They're growing boys. So we opened up our cookie jar."

"We always keep it stocked."

"And that's when their friends came in, Leopold marching right behind them."

"Doesn't it beat all?"

Mayor Corbett jumped in then. "I don't understand. Tugs seemed to think . . ." But Miss Lucy interrupted him, holding up her hand.

"Mayor. I happened to look out the reference materials window this afternoon and saw this . . . ah . . . group of young people going to *visit* the Misses Thompson. I intercepted them for a short chat." She gave the Rowdies a knowing look. "And it turns out they were just going to lead Leopold home. Right, boys? And Bess?"

They all nodded, a bit sheepishly.

"They have agreed to keep an eye out for Leopold from now on, and for the Thompson twins. In fact, they will be back next week to sweep their walk and help with their garden. Won't you, boys? And Bess?"

"Well, then," said Father Button. "I guess we could be moseying along now."

"Oh, don't go yet!" said Elmira. "The party's just getting good."

"And I want to know what happened to your crook, Tugs! Where's your dashing crook What's-His-Name?" said Eldora.

"Mr. Moore," said Elmira. "Also known as Dapper Jack, wasn't that it?"

"Crook?" said Miss Lucy. "Mr. Moore? Dapper . . ."

Tugs looked at her father.

"Go on up to the porch, Tugs. Tell everyone the story."

Tugs threaded her way up the steps past Luther Tingvold and Walter Williams.

"Right here, Tugs," said Miss Lucy, motioning for Tugs to stand in front of the railing. Tugs looked out at the yard, where a small crowd had spilled out of the library, joining the Millhouses, her father, and Mayor

Corbett. Mary Louise and her mother came out of their house to see what the commotion was all about.

Tugs felt shy, but there was her father, and Aggie Millhouse, smiling up at her. She wished Ned were there, too.

"It started when Mr. Moore didn't know our car was out of gas," said Tugs. She paused to compose the sequence of events in her head. "And then he didn't know the way downtown or where his office was. Now that I think about it, he didn't answer to his name when I called out to him, either. He was too nice on the outside, but not at all nice when adults weren't around. I don't know. Something didn't feel right. So I was suspicious of him. And he kept taking money from people. It seemed like a lot of money.

"Then Miss Thompson and Miss Thompson told me about their pictures being in the old newspaper."

"That's us!" squealed Elmira.

"Shhh," said Eldora.

"So I went to the library to look at old newspapers, and I found this article and photograph." Tugs dug in her pocket and pulled out the clipping, folded into a small square. She looked at Miss Lucy. "Sorry, Miss Lucy. I took it out of the paper. Here." Tugs handed it to Miss Lucy.

"Not to worry," said Miss Lucy, studying the photo closely.

"It's about a man named Dapper Jack Door. That's who Harvey Moore is. He goes to towns like ours and makes up stories that make people want to give him money. Then he leaves town with their money, and they don't get anything in return. But Officer Miller has him now, and everyone's money is at the Dostals'. You'll get it back."

"My stars," exclaimed Miss Lucy. "She's right. The likeness in this picture is uncanny. Tugs! If you hadn't noticed this and acted on your suspicions, I just don't know where we'd be." Miss Lucy gave Tugs a hug and addressed the gathering.

"Citizens of Goodhue," she said, "check your clothing. Is anyone wearing a button? Do you know what the meaning of *button* is? It's a fastener, of course. We use ordinary buttons every day.

"But *button* also means 'to bring to a successful conclusion.' And Tugs Button defined that word for us today. I shudder to think! We thought we were going to get a newspaper here. The *Goodhue Progress*. Many of us, myself included, dipped into our resources to make it happen. But all this time a con artist was hoodwinking us. My stars.

"Swindling is not progress. If it weren't for you, Tugs, that scoundrel would have been on his way out of town with our money.

"Some people have a lucky rabbit's foot, or a lucky coin, but here in Goodhue, we have a lucky Button. Tugs Button. Let's hear it for Tugs!"

Everyone clapped. Even the Rowdies

and Mary Louise. The Thompson twins loudest of all.

Tugs waved shyly, then ducked off the porch to stand next to Aggie.

"We should probably go," she said to her father. "Want to come over, Aggie?"

"Sure," she said.

The crowd started to break up. People stopped and patted Tugs on the back and shook her hand as they walked by.

"Wait!" hollered Elmira from the porch.

"Hold up!" Eldora chimed in. The sisters helped each other down the steps and hurried toward Tugs. "Here," they said. "We want you to have this." They each shoved a blue Brownie camera at Tugs.

"I couldn't," said Tugs.

"You can!" they said.

"All right," Tugs agreed. "But just one." She took one of the perfect undented blue Brownies and handed back the other.

"Then your sister can have the other," said Eldora, handing a camera to Aggie.

"We aren't sisters," said Tugs and Aggie, laughing.

"Good as," said Elmira. "Take it anyhow. You'll have more fun together."

"Thank you," said Tugs. "We'll take pictures for you."

"I think Tugs has mine," said Eldora to Elmira.

"I'm quite sure she's got mine," said Elmira, and they teetered back to the porch, where Leopold was just slipping out from between the rails.

Acknowledgements

I am grateful to those who helped me raise this book:

Editor Deborah Noyes Wayshak asked, believed, propelled.

Dan Baldwin made lightning strike during every brainstorm, and Leigh Brown Perkins's keen insight was my flashlight through draft after draft.

A picnic on the Iowa prairie introduced me to Tugs Button and an extraordinary group of bookmakers, the Tall Grass Writers, whose joyful spirit keeps me writing: Michelle Edwards, Carol Gorman, Jacqueline Briggs Martin, and Claudia McGehee.

My mother ignited my passion for books and writing by placing a notebook in my one hand and a library card in the other. That library card led me to my own Miss Lucy, Lucy Selander at the Roosevelt branch of the Minneapolis Public Library. Her power to divine the right book for the right moment enchanted my childhood.